JOHN ROBERTS

Walking Alone

Matador
9 Priory Business Park,
Wistow Road, Kibworth Beauchamp,
Leicestershire. LE8 0RX
Tel: 0116 279 2299
Email: books@troubador.co.uk
Web: www.troubador.co.uk/matador
Twitter: @matadorbooks

ISBN 978 1785892 004

British Library Cataloguing in Publication Data.
A catalogue record for this book is available from the British Library.

Printed and bound in the UK by TJ International, Padstow, Cornwall
Typeset in 11pt Aldine401 BT by Troubador Publishing Ltd, Leicester, UK

Matador is an imprint of Troubador Publishing Ltd

For my Mum

Marjorie Edith Catherine Roberts née Dearden (1917-2008)

and Dad

Norman James Roberts (1915-1969)

*who took us to North Wales for family holidays
for more than a dozen years.*

1. WALK, DAY ONE

Six full Welsh breakfasts, thinks Jack, *before the island, before I decide whether to kill myself. Six meals for the condemned man. Going out in style.*

He sips his orange juice in the empty hotel dining room. Three other tables are laid but he has asked for an early start.

All things considered, weighing it all up, will that be the rational thing to do? And if it is, will I have the guts? Perhaps that's the harder question. And what does that *say about me?*

"Good morning," he greets Nicoletta, the plump, dark-haired Romanian waitress who has found her way to this tiny Welsh village. "I'll have the full Welsh," he says. "Including the hash browns and black pudding. Thanks."

He'll need the energy for the first of his five days of walking. The Welsh breakfast, it appeared from the menu, was the same as an English one: a disappointment. He'd looked forward to laverbread cake: seaweed puree mixed with oatmeal, formed into patties and fried in bacon fat. It would have been appropriate for a coastal walk.

Nicoletta brings him a pot of boiled water into which he drops two of his decaffeinated teabags and stirs them round. The taste is flat and pallid. He dislikes it but ordinary tea, like caffeinated coffee, makes his heart race. He has been so careful with his body for years, followed routines that made him feel safe. Ridiculous in a way to be still cautious but he doesn't want to risk an untimely medical crisis.

Stay healthy to die properly.

His death must be a conscious decision, a predetermined event of his own design.

1

Why be so sombre and melodramatic? I'm looking forward to it – it's why I've chosen to be here, for God's sake! My own carefully engineered anticlimax. Not with a bang but a whimper. Ho, ho!

He tucks into his bowl of muesli and sees, through the window, clouds capping the three summits of Yr Eifl, hills that he will cross next day. A sure sign of rain, the local taxi driver had said, but the sun is shining from an otherwise clear sky. He might be lucky.

It's my turn, muses Jack. *Kathy died by cruel accident, in a car crash.* Kathy was always there, ready to step out of a twilit corner of his mind into the bright sun of a sudden memory. *But mine will be no accident.*

His breakfast arrives, the deep yellow scrambled egg adorned with one incongruous purple salad leaf. *The wheel turns.*

It is the spring of Jack's sixty-seventh year. April –'when longen folk to goon on pilgrimages/ And palmeres for to seken straunge strondsʼ There will not be many 'straunge stronds' during this walk for Jack spent many childhood holidays in these parts, then brought his own children and, last year, his three grandsons. This coast contains his own history: it will be a pilgrimage to memories of his past as well as the dilemma of his future.

He tucks in, looking at the sunshine creating swirls and stripes of different shades of blue on the sea. A white-sailed yacht far away seems to float in the sky, the horizon lost in haze. It could be a good day but he is nervous: he doesn't know how his arthritic knees will cope with the descents or if he will navigate correctly. He will be walking ever south and west along the Lleyn Peninsula, treading in the footsteps of medieval pilgrims to the holy island of Bardsey who, in turn, had followed the sixth century monks and hermits. Jack likes the idea of being part of that peregrination, following a traditional path in the search for truth even though he is an atheist. But he seeks the truth about his real past life, rather than the pilgrims' truth of an imagined afterlife.

Pretentious and grandiose as usual! He almost snorts into his flat, tepid tea and puts the cup back on the saucer. *Christ! Is this tea not penance enough? But I've an OK reason for a pilgrimage. The idea of a godless pilgrimage appeals to me. I'm not looking for a miracle or a cure for my ailments, I'm not here in fear of Judgement Day nor seeking remission for my sins. I'm not a penitent – except for the tea – and I'm certainly not going to be frugal and self-mortifying – except for the tea. I won't be kissing relics and I certainly don't fancy putting my hand into some saint's coffin to mucky my fingers with dust so I can mix it with water and create what's supposed to be a holy medicine.*

Jack knows he needs all the help he can get to reflect on and come to terms with his truth. Feeling rather smug about his own acumen, he'd deliberately chosen the five-day trek rather than the six or four-day versions, because of the connotations of the sacred number five: the pentangle or pentagram with its occult mysteries. He feels he is old enough now to indulge his pretentions and he loved learning that the five-pointed star had been carved in ancient Babylon, was in the cuneiform writing of Mesopotamia and in Egyptian hieroglyphics, that it had featured on Gnostic amulets and for Christians represented the five wounds of Christ. Why should he reject even the most infinitesimal morsel of those magic properties so many generations and cultures had revered and feared? In his own tiny and inconsequential way he sees himself as the fag-end of those rites – rubbing the magic ring, burning incense, chanting incantations, incising runes. *Superstition was always more enticing than religion,* and even as he thinks it, he smiles at his own banality. Too late for him to be granted the wisdom of old age.

He ends his breakfast with three slices of toast, stocking up on carbs, savouring the sweet apricot jam. Then in his bedroom he takes his irbesartan and bisoprolol for his fibrillating heart, his warfarin to help reduce the likelihood of strokes, his glucosamine and chondroitin to protect what little suppleness there remains in his joints, especially his knees and hands, his simvastatin for his cholesterol. Once, at the start, he had hated the pills, he who'd hardly had a day's illness all his life. Then he had become dependent on them for survival, was grateful for them. *Is* grateful for them, at least for a few more days. But it's a tedious ritual.

At least the NHS will be slightly better off. They will benefit from my demise almost as much as my kids, grief assuaged by reduced mortgages.

He stuffs the sachets of pills into a small, yellow pouch. As he packs and fastens his daysack, his fingers cramp up as they are doing more frequently these days. It is not muscle cramp but joint cramp, what a friend gleefully explained – as if welcoming him to an elite club – was the harbinger of arthritis.

He can leave the rest of his luggage in the room as he is staying here a second night. Leaving baggage behind is a symbolic act for pilgrims: abandoning unnecessary burdens such as guilt and lack of self-worth, as well as TV schedules and mobile phones. But there's a limit to sacrifice! There's a Champions League semi-final tonight and he needs the phone to make his taxi contacts. It's one of these walking-for-softies treks where he will be picked up by taxi at the end of the day's walk and brought back to the hotel. Tomorrow the taxi will take his luggage to his next hotel where he will meet up with it after another day's walk.

He is about to pack his phone into the side pocket of his rucksack when he makes a decision. The urge to contact Branwen is one he fights many times. But now he thinks: *why not?* Branwen, the broken dream of a foolish old man, the intense fiction he has lived through in his head while he lived alone, voices of Radio 4 filling the empty room where he ate his solitary lunch of cottage cheese on Ryvitas and stirred his cup-a-soup. Nine and a half years ago, when Kathy was killed, he had felt compelled to phone her – the only person from whom he could seek some solace, a re-assurance at a crucial time in his life. *You are a good man,* she had said immediately, the same Branwen whom he had so callously rejected thirty years before. This trip is his final defining moment. What has he to lose? He suddenly wants her to know he is here, where they walked and loved so passionately in the past, and then briefly renewed when they met again just four years ago. He needs that sense of being with her. So he texts:

Just starting 5 day Pilgrims' Trail to Aberdaron. Next Saturday I sail from there to Bardsey for a week. So much nostalgia. Jack

He does not risk a kiss and presses 'Send'. 'Message sent' comes up on the screen. It is done. As ever, when he sends a text to Branwen, he feels a real contact even though he is resigned that there will be no reply. Feeling vindicated and dissatisfied at the same time, he tucks the phone in beside the small wooden pyramid he will carry: today's section of the sacred geometry of the five Platonic solids, the tetrahedron – a harmony found within the overall folly.

Bloody typical, she'd say. *Default position of your mind is glorified crap!* She'd laugh. How he missed her, three years of silence since their brief reunion. *These fragments I have shored against my ruins, you know, Branwen: something to grasp, or knead.* Fortified with aspects of ritual, each day he hopes will have its pattern and emphasis.

Outside the hotel in the morning sunshine he feels properly prepared: he has the pilgrim's scrip and staff – his daysack and trekking pole. He slings his daysack on his back, plonks on his sunhat and is ready to start on today's miles.

Sitting on the wall outside the hotel is a man having a smoke, shaven-headed as a swami, sandals and grey socks, T-shirt tight over the swell of his stomach, shorts. Jack has a sudden thought and asks:

5

"Can you check for me? What's my pedometer say? It's upside down and I can't read it. I've forgotten if I set it to nought."

The man bends down and peers at the pedometer slotted on Jack's belt.

"Yes, it's at zero. Why are you wearing it?"

"I like to know how much I've done in a day. Some research has recently found that the optimum walking distance per week is ten and a half miles."

"Optimum for what?" asks the smoker.

"Doing that distance is the best way to stave off... er, what's it called? Not Alzheimer's... er, bloody hell, what is the bloody word? Don't tell me!"

"Dementia?" suggests the man.

"That's it, bloody dementia. Well, it's supposed to be staved off."

His first objective is 200 yards away: the church of St Beuno, a major stopping-place for the medieval pilgrims and still huge for this small village of Clynnog Fawr. The crenellations on the church blush pink in the sun, the churchyard is white with hawthorn and pink with flowering cherry. Near the door is a tall, free-standing stone sundial. Dutifully he reads that it is 1,000 years old. It had once been used as a footbridge over a mill-stream in the village and had been found being used as a slab support for milk churns at a farm: a sturdy peasant lack of deference. He sees the empty hole where the gnomon once cast its moving shadow across a semi-circle carved into eight tides for the times of worship. Its absence is satisfying, the loss and removal of things. All things pass. Yet in this church important things have continued, fears and hopes have been muttered, help sought, promises made, failures consoled.

He steps inside the church, his trekking pole tapping the stone-slabbed floor. This empty, silent church echoes with generations: shuffling of feet, murmurings of prayers, songs of praise. Though light with many plain glass windows it is chilled after the sun outside. The main feature is St Beuno's ash chest, hollowed out of a single ash trunk and now protected in a glass case. Jack reads the inscription: 'Here I offer to God 4 pence for my private sins on which account the Almighty is now punishing me.'

Bloody convenient, thinks Jack, *to be able to pay off your sins in the moneybox, to count your rosary beads and say your Hail Marys. A win-win system – the sinner starts again with a clean slate, the prelate can afford a finer glass of wine. They weren't daft, a practical solution to the problem of guilt and weakness.*

He's chilled now and leaves the church to walk a hundred yards up the lane to St Beuno's well. There is an iron gate padlocked by a bright blue bicycle lock. He almost steps into a pile of dried dog shit as he looks over the gate and sees a flight of stone steps. Up there, the guidebook tells him, is a square pool surrounded by an open-roofed stone well house. It is overgrown now with brambles and hawthorn. Two squashed, shiny blue tins of Foster's lager have been thrown onto the steps. He turns away; he must start his walk. A tractor with a muck-spreader rattles past, the pure morning air suddenly smeared with a sharp stink.

Up a steep, narrow, twisting lane he steps at a watchful, steady pace. Doves coo in the churchyard trees below him, buzzards mew above as they circle on thermals. A blackbird scurries out in front of him from behind a yellow salt bin. Gradually, buzzing flies and trickling streams replace the hum of traffic. Jack smiles wryly at the violet heartsease in the grass. *An optimistic symbol? Irony?* He passes a ruined mill with a huge, rusting waterwheel and then the track ends and he is on the open hillside, lambs in the fields scuttering to their mothers in a panic when he appears. It is hot and there is no breeze. He plods on, his heart beating steadily, feeling good. He climbs a stile over the last wall and is finally on the moor. Walking is more strenuous now, big tussocks and a spongy, deep bog sucking his boots in. Up here, alone, he feels an atavistic fear of sinking helplessly into the quagmire, the mud closing over him. Stumbling, hands pointlessly grasping the reeds, he struggles on, aiming for the corner of a wall, a long, straight wall which helps form a huge rhomboid field, cantilevered across the slope of the hill, riding directly over dips and rises, geometrically incongruous. When he reaches it he sits down to rest and waits for his heart to slow. The silence rings in his ears: only the call of a raven circling over Bwlch Mawr. Branwen always with him, Branwen meaning raven in Welsh, her hair black and glossy as a raven's.

Nearby are the remains of a sheepfold, and the far older shapes of hut circles.

He is about halfway through his day's walk, time for lunch. He eats his ham and mustard sandwich, his apple and Kit Kat, drinks his still water. Kathy was his most tragic failure and she remains the core of his life, continuing now in the joy of their daughter, Megan. But Kathy remains also in the sadness of experiences not shared with her. His past is full of ruins, his present filled with guilt and self-contempt: how he behaved with Abi and Tom, with his mother. He will confront these on the middle days of his walk, the three contemplations of his pilgrimage. But, over the week, he will also relive the story of Branwen.

But the first task is to reach today's destination. He shivers, partly because he is now in the shadow of the wall. The sun has moved round and the sweat has dried cold on his T-shirt as he leans back onto the grass.

It was all a long time ago. He works it out: thirty-six years ago. And still he remembers the emotional intensity, racked almost to splitting point. Yet he is envious of his old self. He had been alive, raw to the desolation of losing his children but also open to that first, glorious, urgent, vibrant time with

8

Branwen. Then there had been the reunion with Branwen and now the last three years of his life have been bland, at one remove from real experience, as if he had swallowed an emotional analgesic.

But perhaps that's what the mind did: after the failures with his wife Vicky, then Branwen, and the loss of Kathy, it closed down, mental fatigue. It was a survival tool.

He levers himself up off the grass and glances along the drystone wall that stretches in the direction of the top of Gyrn Ddu. He plods up the remaining 200 feet to the col to meet a footpath that becomes a cart track heading due west. The young bracken fronds are still pale green and furled, coiled like a scorpion's tail, sinister somehow. Or blessed, like a crozier.

Now he can see to the south-west the hills of Yr Eifl that he will cross tomorrow. A heat haze blurs their focus, tints them with lavender. Earlier in the day he had seen lambs, bees, flowers and trees budding. Now on the track he is conscious of derelict farms, of lives finished, walls and dreams broken, passing ruined quarry buildings, inclined trolleyways and the rusted remains of pulley wheels. Below he can see the village of Trefor, the end of his walk, once a place that prospered from the massive granite quarry above it, now mute. He arrives earlier than expected and sits in the sun on the beach. He feels OK, no muscle soreness, no aching knees, chuffed that he has needed no painkillers to ease his way. Plump women sit on the old stone jetty, skirts pulled up above their pink knees, stretching their legs in the sun.

He picks up a pebble from the beach. Each day he will collect an object that is somehow appropriate. The pebble is grey and hard but rounded, eroded by millions of waves and collisions with other pebbles, of no consequence, but proof of the passage of time. He puts it in his pocket. Quite what he will do with the five objects he doesn't know. Will they be a votive offering to the Earth as he bids it farewell? Or an enigmatic collection left on a tray in his cottage kitchen, a disinterested hand sweeping them into a rubbish-bag? Or will he send them as a final present to Branwen, with no explanatory note, just a signature? A poignant riddle that might intrigue or annoy her.

Ah! Branwen – for five years after Kathy's death Megan and I lived our lives together and I had no thoughts of anyone else. Then Megan left for university and I brought you back into my life. With you I have travelled through glories and miseries. I have laughed with you and ached for you. I have hurt you and flattered you. Maybe it wasn't love all those years ago, I was too mixed up for that, led astray by the dancing light of a ship wrecker. But now it is love, and has been for these last four years when my life has centred round your fleeting presence and your long absence.

Have you read my Bardsey text message? Before you deleted it, did you pause for a moment and think softly of me? Or did you just instantly press the key, a flash of irritation disturbing your indifference? I'll never know. Do you ever recall our passion, I wonder, that passion I desecrated?

On this last journey to Bardsey, I want to relive our story, relive my authenticity, walk again in those colours flaring over us like sunlight through stained glass: that time before I became insipid, compelled to take on this drabness to get through. You, after all, are the other reason why I go the island.

*

The first time Jack saw her, Branwen was three places ahead of him in the queue for coffee in the staff canteen: a slim, tallish woman with black hair to her shoulders, animated gestures as she chatted whilst the coffee machine roared like a jet engine. Turning her head, she glanced at him and then back. She'd registered nothing, unlike him.

With their polystyrene beakers they filed into their first team meeting, nine people selected to lead and organise this new approach to aid for developing countries. They were younger than him except for one grey-haired woman who appraised him from across the table. They wrote their names on cards and placed them in front of them. The black-haired woman was Branwen, and the older lady Laura. He felt an expectation in the room, a taut, poised energy. They had all volunteered for the project – drawn to it like himself, assumed Jack, because it involved a vision, one which would have to be fought for against the authorities. He looked forward to the battle against bureaucrats and red tape and status quo complacency within the department. They would have to ruffle feathers.

Sustainability was the core of the project: how to help a village in Africa so that it learned to help itself. Not just handouts of cash and equipment but the training and education of local people to manage and maintain the improvements. This would bring them into conflict with existing power structures over there as well: governmental, regional and local, who were used to lining their own pockets out of aid money. There would be conflicts too about the traditional roles of women.

Jack watched as Branwen spoke about the project they were setting up, her almost-black eyes sparkling with enthusiasm, her face so expressive, smile so captivating, her long, dark hair swinging around her face. They were a team fighting a cause, a principle in action, a fight for the dispossessed against privilege, a fight for fairness. Branwen led that struggle. Their idealism and their sense of being a pioneering minority against the 'powers that be' quickly bonded them all together. As this first planning meeting continued with ideas about village health teams, classroom construction and community radio, Jack wondered if Branwen felt the same attraction to him as he did to her. Was she totally immersed in the discussion or was she aware of him?

At the end of the first day, asking around his colleagues, he was told how hard-working she was, how full of ideas and initiative, a good team player with a lively social life. She generated optimism. Jack knew he was already being drawn in by that and also by her physical vitality. After another day of stimulating discussion, the initiation of action plans, the delineation of obstacles and first ideas as to how they might be overcome, Jack asked Branwen out for a drink. She accepted with a ready smile and for most of the evening continued discussion about the project. Jack grew more confident that she liked him – little touches on his arm, laughter, a brightness in her eyes, a sense of mischief just beneath her serious commitment.

On their second evening out in a pub Jack and Branwen confided that both their marriages were on the rocks. She was a self-made girl, born on a tough council estate in the city, determined to break out and get to university where she'd studied Ecology. She'd married a school boyfriend, kind, content in a job with no career prospects, totally without aspiration. His limitations and her expanding horizons slowly created a gap they could not cross. She tried because she was loyal and dutiful but she could not deny she was bored with him. They had little in common. As she spoke Jack could not help but register the soft, creamy skin of her face and shoulders and bare arms. Then Jack, in turn, told her of the failing attempt to repair his marriage with Vicky, about his children, Abi and Tom, and how Vicky was establishing another relationship with Justin. Branwen listened attentively, did not probe, but he sensed an understanding in her. To speak with so much natural honesty was new to him; Branwen's own honesty and directness released his own.

Outside, as they walked across the dark car park, he turned and kissed her. She responded. It became a lingering kiss and he felt her arms reach around him and hold him. That had been the simple start. Two days later Branwen announced she was leaving her husband: there was nothing left to stay for. Within a fortnight she had moved into a furnished flat while the divorce proceedings were set in motion. During that time Jack and Branwen had walked hand in hand on empty winter beaches, had drinks in country pubs, talked endlessly.

Jack knew that Vicky was seeing more and more of a man called Justin, a counsellor. While Jack spent long hours in extended meetings at work, Justin accompanied Vicky to the park with Abi and Tom, pushing them on swings, speeding up the roundabout. Sometimes he even prepared meals for them. Vicky told him all this quite openly: was she telling him everything was definitely over between them or was it to see if he would rise to the challenge? Jack knew that Justin was giving Vicky the time and attention he himself didn't. In bed together Jack and Vicky didn't talk or touch.

One evening after the kids had gone to bed and Jack had read them a story he came downstairs into the kitchen where Vicky greeted him with the words:

"We need to talk, Jack."

He closed the door and sat down.

"I don't know what you're doing or who with," said Vicky, "and I don't want to know. I think you have someone. But I want a trial separation."

She looked at him straight in the eye. His stomach lurched.

"Is this because of you and Justin?" Jack countered.

"Partly. We've grown very fond of each other, I admit. But it's mainly because of *us*… there's nothing left, is there?"

"Not if you say so."

"No, don't pass the buck to me. We're leading separate lives. We don't speak, we don't do things together, not even as a family. I think you're bored with us. I've tried, Jack, but you haven't tried enough. You haven't fought to keep us together."

Jack slumped into his usual inarticulate, emotional

passivity. Why had he not tried harder? Because it would have been a false effort, done only for the sake of it? They no longer wanted to live together because there were no feelings between them. It was as simple and harsh as that. Now the implications flooded in. He would have to move out of his home because Abi and Tom must stay. How could he not be with them? Not see them? Where would he stay?

"And what if I don't go?" asked Jack.

"Then I will go, and take Abi and Tom with me. I'll find a place."

"No, that's not possible," stated Jack. "When would I be able to see the kids?"

"Whenever you want. This is a trial separation. Justin's not moving in, you know."

Jack could not think clearly: his mind was a confusion. This awful emptiness would be over, he would be free to see Branwen more often, but he would be only a visitor to his children.

"What will you tell Abi and Tom?" he asked.

"That you're away doing some special work."

"You've thought it through, haven't you?" said Jack.

"No, not really. I just know I can't go on like this. You don't love me any more. We circle each other, pass each other. We never speak about anything that's important."

Jack knew it was true. He hadn't had the courage to say it. Perhaps Justin gave her the courage. He wasn't moving in, she'd said – yet. But she must have that in mind. It was inevitable.

He found himself saying: "I'll go after breakfast tomorrow. It's Sunday and I can pack some clothes and books and things."

He went upstairs, paused for a long time outside the children's bedroom, pushed open the door a little to look at them, both with thumbs in their mouths, little arms stretched up beside their blonde heads. What was happening couldn't

14

be true. But he went into the main bedroom, took a case from the top of the wardrobe, opened drawers carefully so as not to wake Abi and Tom, and began mechanically to pack. He put the case in the car so they would not see it in the morning. The following day, after breakfast, he left to stay with friends, promising to see the kids at bedtime and read them their favourite story, *The Very Hungry Caterpillar*.

A couple of weeks later, after the pub, Branwen invited him back to her flat. They went to bed: it was the beginning of a period of sexual excitement which neither he nor she had experienced before. It was a revelation: their mutual abandon, their pleasuring of each other. Even some weekday lunchtimes they would drive away from the office to her bedroom, draw the curtains and in the dimmed afternoon light make love with a passion and lack of reticence that was new to both of them. Their passion was somehow part of their highly charged cause. During the day they organised the digging of wells and the setting-up of a local water and sanitation committee, the establishment of a village savings and loan association. By night they explored each other's bodies, the giving and accepting of pleasure.

"With my husband I used to think I was frigid," she confided to him once, her head resting on his chest, her fingers resting companionably around his dozing, satisfied penis.

"Poor thing," she said, cradling his penis in her palm. "Have I tired you out?"

"I wouldn't believe you except that I never believed sex could be like this, either. I'd wondered what all the fuss was about. Now I know."

Jack told her about the awkwardness of his one long-term relationship with Vicky, the unimaginative coupling which never improved but had produced two wonderful children.

One lunchtime in bed, Branwen had been angry with him as she felt him approaching his climax too soon.

15

"No, not yet," she had begged him, "wait for me."

But he had come, unable to control himself, and he had loved her for her anger, her honesty, her wanting to be with him.

"I want to watch you make yourself come," he had said, as the idea spontaneously surfaced in his mind from he knew not where.

To his delight, she had watched him mischievously as he had watched her, fascinated as her finger circled and rubbed and her back had arched and she had moaned in that delicious way she had. And that had aroused him again and he had had to go back into her and this time they had come together. During this time both had exulted in their complete lack of inhibition, able to talk about what they wanted, experimenting with positions, buying each other surprise presents of massage oil and body chocolate. He ran a bath for her, poured in fragrant, relaxing oils, lit candles and gave her a glass of champagne and her book.

One evening Branwen came out of the bathroom into the living room wearing a long black silk dressing gown. When Jack loosened the silk belt and slipped the gown off her shoulders she was wearing only a narrow black choker with an old-fashioned brooch attached to it at her throat, a black leather belt with a large shining metal buckle, long black gloves and black high heels. It blew Jack's mind.

"I almost didn't dare," she said. "Nearly lost my nerve."

"I love it," he said, stroking the length of her.

With a half-real, half-pretend shyness she said:

"I like showing myself off to you. You're so appreciative. You give me confidence. I love to arouse and please you."

She held him and began to stroke him, attentive, careful, as if she were crafting and shaping a figurine – handiwork, in fact. She kissed him and then knelt down. His moans of pleasure fuelled her skills and she began to circle him with her tongue until she knew he was desperate for her to take him into the hot wetness of her mouth. She sucked the length of him, triumphant as he groaned with pleasure. He loved that acceptance of him. Then she stopped and he turned to stroke her. But she said:

"No, this is your night."

She sat astride him, his penis along the groove of her vagina. She leaned forward and brushed her breasts over his mouth, pushed each of her nipples in turn into his mouth. When she leaned back he cupped her breasts in his hands. Then she turned around, still crouched on him, so he could see her insert his penis into her and she rose and fell on him and he watched the arching of her back, the swell of her arse. Again she stopped and turned to take his penis, wet with her juice, into her mouth. Then she knelt over him again, this time facing him because she knew he loved to watch her come – and she loved him to watch her come – and he entered her and they rocked together and each cried out as they shuddered to a glorious climax.

Not long after that, Branwen invited him to move in with her. Jack arranged a weekend in the Lake District. He loved the hills and she loved the exercise and the fresh air. On the Saturday they walked up past an old corn mill out onto the hillside to some old peat houses, most now in ruins, from which they could see Sellafield nuclear power plant. They searched and found stone circles from 2,000 BC, one named Brat's Hill, looked back to the Irish Sea and Morecambe Bay. It looked misty but they pushed on over the rise and angle down to Miterdale and followed the stream up to Burnmoor Tarn before returning by the old corpse road over the moors from Wasdale and ending at the little simple church by the riverside.

In the evening they had an outrageously expensive meal at a sophisticated restaurant overlooking the river. They discussed the walk as Branwen rested her hand on his thigh, looking at him with her provocative, cheeky eyes in which he saw the prospect of mutual pleasure. For him, there was another level of significance in sex: yes, the letting go, the shamelessness, the exploration, the intimacy, the fun. But also for him that momentary, mutual, exquisite loss of self while inside her was their simultaneous connection with the great surge of nature. Even as he thought it, he felt ridiculous and pretentious. But it was true: only with her had he sensed this – a revelation and a homecoming, a completeness newly discovered.

So they walked back to the hotel, arms around each other's waists, along the riverbank. They paused to look at the floodlit medieval facades of the church, their windows reflecting the buildings on the side they stood on, the double reflections caught in the water, two faces of the lit clock on the church tower pinned like two moons between the triangles of the reflected gables. Two bicycles leaned against the railings in silhouette. The curve of a bridge over the river was reflected like a Japanese moongate. The air was still and warm, a couple strolled past enjoying quiet laughter. A cyclist rode by, scarf flying, a church bell struck the quarter hour.

"It's beautiful," said Branwen.

"Yes," he said. He too loved the beauty but also loved the idea that he had brought them here, his initiative, his decision. He was totally happy. He turned and kissed her and she grinned as she felt his erection growing against her.

"And so to bed," she said.

Later, after they had made love, Jack watched Branwen's face as she slept, tenderly stroked her forehead and cheeks, her skin smooth as pearl, with the backs of his fingers. Her lips, slightly open, were so full and sensuous. Through the open bedroom window he heard the clattering of high-heeled shoes on the cobbled lane two floors below, subdued voices and girls' laughter, high-pitched and brash and challenging. Then the noise receded into silence as he listened.

He owed so much to her. She had taken him out from under his shadows and into the sun. The emptiness inside him was filling. She was, just by being herself, clearing away that distrust, dislike of himself, which prevented him from getting close to anyone, always kept him at one remove from someone. The awful daring of a moment's surrender.

"I have come home," he whispered to her and kissed her lightly on her belly. He loved to lie there, feeling her pulse beating, the occasional gurgling of her stomach, his hand resting on her inner thigh.

She stirred and snuggled closer, still asleep.

"I have come home," he repeated to himself.

One Saturday he took his children to the beach. Tom went off crabbing with his net, Abi collecting pebbles and shells to take home to her Mum. Jack stood by a breakwater and watched her scuffing a bedraggled line across the sand as she dragged the bag along. Then she dropped the bag and began to skip and dance along the beach, waving her arms, circling round, making patterns in the sand with her feet. Above him, in a clutter of white wings, seagulls were semaphoring the sunlight. The grey tide washed in with quiet waves. Abi and Tom had been born out of what he had thought was love. Now they were the only repositories of that love, all other aspects of it had died. How much did they understand? How much did they hurt? How would Justin alter their lives and values? He, Jack, was responsible for all these questions. Vicky had been right: he hadn't tried hard enough. Yet Abi was dancing and Tom was absorbed in his crabbing, racing towards him now with a slopping bucket containing his captured crabs. Kids are resilient, they say. Jack must believe it. He was haunted by the fear that he had damaged them. So he played with them, his cheerfulness

19

masking his melancholy, and took them to the beach café for bacon butties and banana milkshakes.

After a particularly hard week on the project, the authorities being more than usually obstructive, Jack and Branwen needed to escape the frustrations. He quickly booked a hotel at a small village on the coast. They left straight from work, Branwen in a bold red coat, her hand resting gently on his thigh. She knew her smile and her moist lips tantalised him.

They drove without talking, the tensions of work draining away and being replaced by anticipation. The road wound round the broad slopes of heather-covered moors, passed large conifer plantations and then came down to the river. But as they finally descended to the fishing village, rain began to fall from the grey clouds that had gradually been banking up all the evening.

Jack had booked the hotel unseen. As they parked the car he saw it was more of a local pub with grey pebble-dashing and peeling window frames. Definitely down at heel. His mood slumped.

"This isn't what I wanted," he said. "It was supposed to be special."

Branwen held his hand. "It doesn't matter, Jack, it will still be special," she said.

Their room was functional and cold, beige wallpaper and small, nondescript pictures marooned on otherwise empty walls, graceless utilitarian furniture. There was a bath but no shower. At least there was a double bed and not twins but the coverlet was dark and heavy, the mattress hard.

Jack flung the suitcase on the bed and turned on the radiator.

"Bloody Calvinistic!" he said. "Let's go for a walk before dinner."

"But it's raining."

"I know that but I need some fresh air."

They walked arm in arm around the stone harbour, out

along the jetty and looked down at the fishing boats. There was no wind and the rain was that ceaseless drizzle that dourly insinuated itself into every tiny gap, soaking into fabric, however waterproof it was designed to be.

Branwen, still bright and sprightly, laughed, leaned her head against his damp shoulder, pointed to a shrieking band of oystercatchers with their long, bright-red bills. Jack saw only the huddle of grey cottages, the grim sea, tasted the cold rain on his lips. A huge herring gull with that blood spot on its yellow bill hurled abuse at them from a granite wall as they passed. It all seemed like a judgement on him. What was he doing here? He should be with his kids, helping with their tea, choosing a book to read with them, cuddled warm with them in their bed. All the simple promise of the weekend was now confused and complicated.

"Let's go back to our cosy hotel," he said, sarcastically. It was more a command than a suggestion.

They went straight to their room. They took off their wet coats and Jack flung himself down on the bed.

"What a shit of a mess," he said, staring at the cracked plasterboard of the ceiling.

"But we're here together," said Branwen, hanging her red coat on the hook behind the door.

She came over and knelt on the bed, leaned forward and kissed his forehead.

"Don't spoil it, Jack."

She kissed him lightly on the lips but he did not respond. She lay down beside him, snuggled into his shoulder and put an arm over his chest. She kissed his ear and blew gently into it. She knew he found that very arousing, like sucking on his finger. He felt her hand move down from his chest to his stomach, her fingers rest on his penis. He felt it inevitably respond. He wrenched himself away.

"No!"

It was an instruction. He sat on the edge of the bed.

"Jack, there's no need for all this."

He walked over to the window and looked out at the wet street. *It's wrong, it's meaningless,* he thought. *I'm hurting my kids, now I'm hurting her.*

"Jack, please lie down. Let's talk about it."

He stayed where he was. The street was empty. He heard the muffled sound of a radio in the room next door. A toilet flushed.

"There's nothing to talk about. It's just fucking guilt. I can't deal with it."

"I understand," said Branwen. "But do you ever imagine what I feel when you say that?"

The truth was that it had never crossed his mind. There was silence.

"I'm hungry," he said.

"Me, too," she said immediately, hoping that something normal might help. A full stomach always put Jack in a better mood. Seeking some reconciliation – something shared, at least, he thought – they went down to the bar. But the dining room was shut, there were only bar snacks.

"This gets better and better," said Jack.

"It doesn't matter," replied Branwen and they ordered chicken and chips and two pints. That she drank beer was one of the things he liked about her.

"We'll go back tomorrow," Jack announced.

"But we're supposed to be staying for the weekend. We're booked in."

"I don't care. It's not working out."

"It's because you're tired. You've had a hard week and a long drive and the weather's miserable. We'll be OK, it will get better. I promise."

"It's more than all that. It's not as straightforward as I thought. It's not you."

22

They sat together in silence. Two old men were at the far end of the bar, each with a whisky. They muttered occasionally to each other as they played dominoes. The barman was drying glasses. The round tables and chairs were empty, the room shabby, the floor scuffed.

"I'm sorry about upstairs," Jack said.

He wanted to kiss her for her understanding but something held him in check. That night they slept together in the hard double bed. They did not make love, they lay estranged. Slowly he felt her disappointment turn to resentment. He lay awake in the dark in this anonymous room, conscious of her lovely, loving, young, warm body only inches away, how he had hurt her, but he was full of doubt and self-recrimination.

The sun shone and cloud shadows dappled the gentle hills as they drove home next day. The car handcuffed them for the long journey. They hardly spoke. Jack was in a mass of confusion again: guilt and fear about Abi and Tom, guilt over treating Branwen so badly. It had all gone so wrong. Each wanted so much to please but he had failed.

But the weekend faded and they tried to re-establish themselves. They decided it was a one-off. Not long after that, they had what became the fatal conversation. Branwen spoke of wanting children – something essential for her. But Jack told her he would have no more children – he had done sufficient damage to Abi and Tom and could not risk repeating it. Branwen questioned his faith in them as a couple. Jack denied it. Their voices rose to their first row and then softened. She didn't want children now, she said quietly, but in the not-too-distant future. She didn't want to be a middle-aged mother. But Jack was adamant: he was terrified of the idea. The conflict shadowed the following days. A distance grew between them and a silence fell. They became estranged in their lovemaking. There was an unbridgeable gap. Trust and their natural ease with other had gone, and their faith in

23

a future together. Jack began staying overnight at a friend's house. Branwen withdrew into herself. They began to avoid each other in the offices of the project. Each hurt and was hurt and neither could make the first move to a reconciliation.

Buoyed by his new sexual confidence, with Branwen placing demands on him that he could not meet, still living with an emotional intensity in the aid project where their ideas were now facing substantial opposition – now it was that Jack made what he would later call the second biggest mistake of his life. He had learned nothing from the break-up of his marriage. He began to respond to the attention being paid to him by Laura, another woman on the project. They talked at coffee time and he learned she was divorced with two children. She was only five years older than him.

Later, in an attempt to justify himself, he would understand that he confused what was in the times with what was in his own nature. What was in the times was embodied in some way in Laura, and it was alluring. Her ready, rippling laughter mocked authority and dismissed gravitas; her long, free-flowing, prematurely grey hair defiantly advertised an unconventional individual; the long, rough-textured, ethnic, earthen-coloured skirts and yin-yang earrings approved an alternative lifestyle of occasional pot, folk guitar, casual but not promiscuous sex, temporary commitment.

She was the older woman, wise counsellor, guru, who proudly showed him the candlelit shrine of marigolds and small, unglazed, brown clay figures that she had created in the attic bedroom of her fisherman's cottage, a room hung with tapestries and crammed with books of poems and eastern philosophy and Carl Rogers' alternative psychology. Even then Jack thought it sad, almost pathetic, as if she was caught in a time warp, yet somehow still enticing.

He sensed but denied to himself a very conscious theatricality and posturing on her part. Laura was karma,

24

experimental, bohemian, exotic, let-it-all-hang-out – so far as the boy from his conservative suburban home was concerned. She was part of the same world as the American poet he met who lived an open marriage and told him she only orgasmed after completing a poem. These were aspects of a life he stood nervously on the outside of but found fascinating. He had read about it in books like *Do It* and in the Beat poets. It was a revisitation of the sixties he had lived through and completely missed in his respectable, marriage-regulated, career-forming life. She was also part of the rich, socially adept, arty elite of the local TV channel. Laura was a seductive cocktail and Jack succumbed.

So, cruelly, brutally, he and Laura played out their games in full view of Branwen. He moved out of the flat permanently. Branwen never pleaded or remonstrated with him, never sought an explanation, strong-willed to the end. She washed her hands of him, simply resigned from the project and moved to another city. Jack and Laura slept together a few times and Jack was surprised to find how conventional Laura was in bed, boring even. In a few weeks their affair was over and Jack was alone. How clever and deliberate he felt Laura had been: too late he realised her obsessive need to appear to be top woman, to compete with and defeat Branwen for the sake of it. Jack had been duped. In Branwen he had thrown a pearl away. He had chosen the superficial over the real.

By now Justin and Vicky were living together and Jack was a desperate part-time father, Abi and Tom living with a usurper. He was on his own. Through his weakness he had lost everything. Only two months later the project collapsed. The authorities, suspicious and uncertain of what their approach might unleash, had withdrawn funding. The team broke up. Jack was truly alone.

★

Enough! That first instalment is sufficient for the day. A few months on which my life turned – and Branwen's, too. So vivid, still. Branwen found a deeper happiness when she married two years later – but me? Yes, for a time.

It was a story he had gone over many times since they had met again four years ago, thirty years after those events. At each retelling he had had to confront his cruelty to her and the grossness of his mistake. It was a pointless pastime: he couldn't rewind the tape. As she was later to tell him: "Perhaps, after all, we have each lived the life fitting for us."

But he felt intensely nostalgic for the richness of that time – for the mix of idealism and sensuality he had found in Branwen. In their work they had been pioneers – what they had started had now become mainstream. And in their love, they had discovered new parts of themselves.

Nevertheless, without that mistake he would not have loved Kathy and would not have Megan. Contortions there, too. The path of his life was twisted and convoluted – somehow leading to sitting alone on this pebbly beach in Gwynedd in bright sunshine beneath a closed-down quarry. A sudden image of Kathy catches his breath: how, barefoot, she loved to run in the shallow tide, carrying her sandals in one hand, holding Megan in the other, the two of them, splashing and laughing, hair blown in the breeze, sun on their faces.

Enough! I need a hot bath, a meal and that Champions' League match. A reality he can deal with.

He phones the taxi, which soon arrives to pick him up.

"You'll be staying on Bardsey, I hear," says the taxi man.

"Yes, for a week. Should be interesting," replies Jack.

"Don't fancy it myself. Islands make you insular."

"Suppose they do," says Jack.

Each man is an island, he thinks, knowing it's one of his tedious mantras with which he bores his children and friends.

The taxi seats are sticky with heat, the radio is on low,

some woman bleating a song. Jack feels emotionally exhausted but physically he feels good – his skin warmed by sun, his legs pleasantly tired, looking forward to a shower and thirsty for a cool beer.

Marks out of ten for the first subject of contemplation? thinks Jack. *Give it five, neither one thing nor the other. Typical me: a safe, average start. But for Branwen it must be a minus score.*

Back at the hotel he texts Megan that he has survived the first day. She responds immediately: *Congratulations! Keep going!*

2. WALK, DAY TWO

His knees creak as he comes down the hotel stairs next morning, they're already complaining and more will be asked of them today. *Yes, I know it's a test but it's in a good cause,* thinks Jack, *at least that's what I'm hoping. Making peace with myself so I can take my leave – is it possible or is it another of my fantasies?*

Other than his knees, Jack feels in good form. Yesterday's walking was a positive start. The sun shone and he came through the first of his relivings, giving himself some credit, eventually, maybe, of sorts. It seems laughable, now that he was actually doing it, to give his past behaviour marks out of ten, like a schoolteacher. Nor does he believe a pattern will emerge that would give some sort of meaningful progression to his life. Perhaps all he wants is to give himself a last, luxurious reminder – painful and piercing by necessity – of times when he had been fully alive. For even when he failed, had he not failed with feeling? He had lived a full emotional life, no holds barred – was that not something to be proud of? To have been in the gutter and on the clouds? But how could he be proud of something that hurt the people he most loved? Round and round goes his mind.

He hopes he will walk off the aches. Today he has the hexahedron in his rucksack, a cube with its six solid, equal faces, which represents the earth. There is more earth for him to climb today, earth with a known and a legendary history. There is still no wind but it's a grey day. Last night he had watched the clouds build up and douse the sunset, a warning of rain.

He bids farewell to Nicoletta and gets into the taxi, which

28

takes him to the start of the walk, Trefor, where he ended yesterday.

"I can see some blue sky," says Jack, twisting to look out to sea.

"Aye, if you know where to look," says the driver. He drops Jack at the edge of the village. "I'll take your luggage on to your next hotel. Have a good day."

Jack looks up the narrow tarmacked track, an 800 foot climb in three-quarters of a mile. A thin mist conceals the three peaks but Jack remembers from his past walks that the path is a clear one. He sets himself a deliberate, slow, steady pace so he will reach the top of the pass without being breathless.

Like a fucking tortoise these days. Carrying my damaged heart is like carrying a bird's egg in the palm of my hand – so easily dropped or cracked. Delicate, needing care. So bloody frustrating!

He plods up, the tarmac ending; high, untrimmed hedges enclose him as the now muddy, rutted track continues to climb. He comes to a five-barred gate tied with orange baler twine to a tall slice of slate that acts as a gatepost. He opens it and passes through. Just beyond is what looks like the final cottage – grey stone, empty window spaces, part of a breeze block wall at the back, bags of sand and cement half sheltered by a tarpaulin, a cement mixer. But the roof of slates is shiny new. He peers in the doorless doorway, sees the fresh, creamy-brown rafters of the new roof. Coming round to the front of the cottage he looks at the view. Beyond the small, hedged fields, overgrown with patches of rushes, are the roofs of other, lower cottages, the grey village of Trefor below, the bay sweeping round in a graceful bow, a white line of breaking waves quivering. The only sound is the buzzing of flies. He picks a tuft of grey sheep's wool from a strand of barbed wire – his token of the day.

Could I live here, alone at the top of the lane? No. What would I be wary of? The need to be self-sufficient, to be able to solve problems – a

29

stormy winter's night, wind battering at the walls, and something loose and banging, needing to go out into the black with a torch, investigate and put right. I'm not that sort of practical man, I need tradesmen waiting at the end of a phone. And the loneliness – I love it now, passing through, but the silence of dusk and shadows thickening, no one knowing if I'm collapsed on the floor or lying on the couch, my heart for some reason racing, having to wait it out on my own, deal with the panic. All my life I've successfully avoided those tests of self-reliance.

The mists are thinning above him. As he starts up the final section he feels he's not doing too badly, walking on his own – but he's glad of his mobile, the network coverage which exists most of the time, the waiting taxi, the warm shower and the evening meal, people expecting him, knowing his route.

Plastic, I've always been made of plastic, not the real deal. What adventures I've had have been on other folks' coat-tails – friends taking me ice climbing or sea cliff climbing. Trekking in Ladakh with a group. Never on my own, never bivvying alone on a high hill. Never really testing myself. There's no mystery to it: I'm just a coward.

Not like Tom: setting off to Spain after college with his guitar, no job, no Spanish, no contacts. Facing up to things, making it through on his own. Or like Abi, rejecting the Sixth Form, reaching university in her own, independent way via part-time jobs and night school.

Weirdly comforted by this conclusion, he plods up to the high point of the track. The mist has gone, just a few last drifting streamers on one peak, the peak of the Giants' Fortress. He notices the thin footpath that contours round the hill before climbing up there. He remembers last summer when he had climbed it, slowly and with the help of his trekking pole, with his three children and three grandsons aged six and four and one. There were frequent halts to coax the boys up with chocolate and cereal bars and for him to husband his resources. Tom had

30

been carrying baby Pete on his back. At the top of Tre'r Ceiri, the Giants' Fort, in the blowing wind, Tom had wanted a photo.

"I like our three generations being together," he had said.

And so the photos were taken (Jack had a print at home on the bookshelf top), Jack smiling, ruefully aware that Tom was already collecting family memorabilia for when he, Jack, was dead.

"That's Grandad," Tom would later say. "Do you remember him, Pete?"

What would Pete reply?

Jack sighs again. There was no avoiding it, life is a sad business: a series of partings, of paths leading away, and absences that rehearsed the final parting but made it no easier. Photographs on the tops of shelves or pianos were usually of people who were absent, not present. His own collection was of his great-grandparents whom he had never known, his grandparents, parents, uncles, aunts – all dead, passed on, as they say. And Kathy: the greatest gap of all. Photos of his children, too, moved away to their separate, independent lives, and his grandchildren. It was all right and proper, the natural way of things, the turn of the wheel. Soon, photos of him would be added to his children's collection, occasionally glanced in passing. No photograph of Branwen in his collection, though. That was his secret life. Only in her own web of lives did she exist, never a part of his. It had been his greatest sadness for four years or so.

He looks round: land falls gradually in front of him, another bay opens out, the peninsula stretches ahead. He can see the sea on both sides of it, the rise of sudden smaller hills from the flat farmland. And there, a white smudge on a narrow promontory, are the low cottages and pub of Porthdinlleyn, where he will walk tomorrow.

He remembers Kathy, swearing at herself and cursing him for the pointless folly of it all as she scrambled up the exposed shoulder of Pen-y-Ghent. She was terrified, grimly clinging to the rocks, white-knuckled. But she never gave in. 'Nae feart!' as a Scots friend had once told him. Then, at the mountain top, her sense of achievement, flinging her arms around him, thanking him for taking her there, loving the moors and mountain landscape.

Now the descent is harder on his knees. Occasionally one gives way, nothing he can foresee or forestall, and he lurches forward, thankful for his trekking pole. Again he must pace himself. He has learned that, above a certain pace, his knees are vulnerable; below it, they can cope. His body has learned the exact degree of incline when he must slow or angle his hips to avoid discomfort. Always adapting, compromising, accepting new limits – that's what ageing was all about: the accumulation of aches, not wisdom. He takes the steep, winding road down the valley to the coast. He had walked down here as a boy, leaving his parents and siblings having a picnic in the car park, when the road was just a track and the line of cottages was in ruins. Even then he must have been drawn to the sadness of forsaken, lonely places.

At a bend on the switchback road he sits on the new stone wall. Below to his left is a thick wood and beyond it the sea. He can just pick out the escarpment shape of Holy Island on Anglesey, or Mon. Ahead of him across the valley are the disused quarries he had passed at the col, the straight inclines cutting like tangents across the hill. His map tells him that, long before quarries, there were ancient field systems, house platforms and hut circles here. This place appeals to his imagination: it contains legend, history, mystery, aspiration and rebirth. This is Nant Gwrtheyrn, the valley of Vortigern, where the last British king ended his days. Betrayed by his Saxon allies, he retreated here, a broken man. This, too, is the valley thrice cursed by the monks when the heathen villagers

32

refused to have a church built here. Here also is a tragic love story: it was the custom for a bride to feign coyness and run away on her wedding morning to hide at a place special to the pair. The groom would seek and find her and bring her to the wedding. On one such occasion the bride ran away but the groom could not find her. He never fell in love again. Years later in a great storm he sheltered under their favourite oak tree. Lightning split the tree and inside, the horrified man found the skeleton of his bride, still in her wedding dress. He died of a broken heart.

It's the tragedy at the core of life that gives those stories their appeal, we recognise it.

Jack wonders if all places have such a rich folklore waiting to be unearthed or if this is an atypical weaving of stories. All things are layered: the earth and its rocks, the land and its hunting/gathering and tillage, the brief lives lived upon it with their few moments of tranquillity – his own life, too: linear, yes, from birth to death, not in a straight line, but zigzagging from elation to melancholy via women and children. Stoic tranquillity – he supposes that means the stage he is at now: learning to appreciate but not desire, learning to put up with rather than change, shifting from active to passive.

Time to bloody move on!

He continues his descent to what is now the Welsh language centre, a place reborn from the ruined cottages he had visited many years ago. It's a testament to the faith and will of a few people determined to maintain their distinctive culture and language. They are dead but their achievement prospers. There's a visitor centre in which he learns that there used to be three quarries here, each with its own pier. He goes over to the newly built café for a coffee and Welsh cakes. Through the huge picture window he is startled to see a group of young Asian women strolling down the path to the viewpoint on the edge of the coast, wearing long black skirts and brown headscarves, carrying handbags: an Islamic retreat on the Christian Pilgrims' Way at the Welsh language centre in a place of ancient British legend.

Fragmented confusion or enriching diversity? I'll go for the enriching, for the moment.

He shoulders his rucksack and leaves. Making for the beach, he passes the young Asian women, chatting and laughing with each other. The path rises from the beach to the cliff top, winding through bushes of brilliant yellow gorse, and then descends by a stream to a complex set of old stone pens and enclosures where pied wagtails flit about. From there Jack can just see his lunch stop – the church at Pistyll. He approaches it with anticipation, as the old pilgrims would have, ready for a rest and a meal after the climbing. Bare feet, sandalled feet would have padded along this path, wooden staves tapping on the dried earth or sticky with mud; now there are trekking boots and poles. He rounds a small hill and there by a stream in the wooded glade is the twelfth-century church. A white chimney sweep's van is parked by the gate, the chimney sweep is cutting the grass, an opened can of Bulmer's cider and his jacket on a stone bench. The mower's petrol fumes hang in the air, its engine snarling among the slanted gravestones and their shadows across the cut, sunlit grass.

The church is dark inside and cool. He eases down onto a pew, glad to get the weight off his feet, the stress off his knees. There are no windows in the north sea-facing wall, apart from a lepers' window near the altar. There's a twelfth-century stone font with Celtic designs – overlapping circles carved around the basin, a scalloped rim and a double row of beading. Jack traces the patterns with his fingers, feeling the grain of the cold stone, hoping for a sense of time to seep through his skin: St Beuno founded a church here fifteen hundred years ago. The stone floor is strewn with rushes.

So many baptisms and benedictions, so much supplication. Some would believe that prayers were answered, others that their sins had still not been exonerated and therefore excused God's failure to help. God won both ways.

Jack returns to the sunshine. The mower and his van have gone, only the now empty cider can remains. Jack sits on the stone bench and stretches his legs out. Beyond the churchyard is a farm with outbuildings. In the guidebook he reads that once this farm was excused its tithes because it offered hospitality to pilgrims. There used to be a monastery here and a hospice, and an extensive range of huts on the field, still called Eisteddfa: place of rest. It would have been a bustling, smelly, noisy, argumentative place, like a market, as traders sought the pilgrims' cash. *No doubt chicanery as well.* Jack unwraps his sandwiches – plain white bread with ham and tomatoes. An appropriate place for a contemplation.

*

In the early October evening, as the light faded and an east wind blew in from the sea, Jack had tramped the length of High Street, from his furnished room in Scholes Place past Mersey Street to Pool Street. Display lights were on in closed shops, buses passed with huddled figures in lighted windows. A pub door opened onto a warm lit bar but he refused the blur of alcohol, he wanted to experience his disconnection defined and undisguised.

He turned into the road where he used to live and where his family still lived. There was no one about; the houses were silent in the dark, the shrubs still and sombre in the gardens. He hesitated two doors away and saw the curtains of his front room drawn, light fringing the edges, made his decision. He moved to his gate, clicked the latch and opened it, the hinges on the old wood creaking. Carefully he closed it.

He moved along the shadowed path to the porch and

stopped. He could not see into the room through the lighted gaps in the curtains but he could hear muffled laughter, *Sergeant Pepper's Lonely Hearts Club Band*, and lively conversation. He moved around the corner and leaned against the house wall; the cold of the brick – solid, thick, unyielding – seeped into his back. Somewhere in there, just the other side of this wall, were his children, in pyjamas ready for bed, playing and being played with: Abi maybe serious with her thumb in, Tom joking and asking eager questions. Soon they would go to bed and Justin would read them their bedtime story.

Jack crouched down on his haunches, the cold now also drawn in from the paving stones through the soles of his shoes. The window of the kitchen door was only a few feet away, the light shining out of it onto the shed. Shadows slid across it as people passed with wine or dishes of food. Bloody hummus, he supposed. He pulled his anorak hood over his head as a fierce draught of the wind was sucked into the narrow gap between the houses, and stared unseeing into the black mass of the rhododendrons he had planted not long ago, their dark leaves heavy and lolling, rasping dryly in the gust.

He broke. Heaving and convulsed with sobs, he moaned a low, attenuated "No, no, no," for all that he had lost, for what he had brought on himself by his own short-sighted selfishness, for not knowing how he would cope.

As his sobs slowly subsided he had a sudden flashing picture of himself: crouched in the dark passage by his house, hooded and weeping, alone, full of self-pity and self-recrimination. While inside, another man – warm, surrounded by friends, his neck casually caressed by Vicky – comforted and joked with his children, all oblivious of him. Was there a greater loneliness?

A week later, Jack unlocked the front door of his house. He knew it would be empty: it was the morning Vicky took Abi and Tom to playgroup. He was there to collect some of his clothes, some books and records. The day he had been terrified of had finally come: he was moving out for good.

He walked slowly through the lounge and dining room and kitchen. Justin's long black coat was slung over the back of an armchair. The rooms were untidy with the kids' toys lying about – books, crayons on the table. Their drawings and paintings were blu-tacked to the walls. The silence overpowered Jack – the temporary absence of Abi and Tom's lively noise and curiosity. The house seemed abandoned by them. He saw that this was his future: like the room now, bereft and empty of them.

He stopped at the top of the stairs, looked at the closed door of the kids' bedroom. He turned aside, just able to keep himself in check, controlled. In the room that he and Vicky had shared he quickly threw some clothes into his rucksack, snatched some favourite books from the shelf, deliberately noticed – as if mortifying himself – that on the bedside table were some of what could only be Justin's books: *The Psychology of Love* and *Gormenghast*. Jack snorted.

Back on the landing, with his rucksack heavy on one shoulder, he held the handle of his children's bedroom door. Little light on this grey day came through the landing window. He waited for a minute, with eyes closed, breathing deeply, his heart thumping. Then he turned the handle and went in. He saw their single beds with rumpled bedclothes, Abi's red wellies in the corner, the mobile by the window, more drawings pinned on the wall, the small sweaters and shorts scattered on the floor.

He threw himself onto Abi's bed, buried his head into her bedclothes, clutched her pyjamas to his face, sought her smell. He grabbed Tom's night T-shirt from his bed and covered his head in their clothes, holding them tight around him with his hands clasped behind his head. Pounding himself into the bed, writhing and kicking his legs violently, he shouted "No, no, no!" He sobbed until he was empty and drained.

In a kind of trance he went back into Vicky's bedroom and took three lipsticks from the dressing table, choosing the richest and deepest reds he could find. Back in the kids' bedroom he began to cover the walls with great scrawls of lipstick, writing over and over again "I love you, I love you." He shouted the words as he wrote, ferociously pressing the lipstick as deep as he could into the wallpaper. When he had ground the lipsticks down to their holders and there was no more to write with he stopped, stood and looked around at what he had done. He was filled with a terrifying despair. Would Abi and Tom understand? How would Vicky and Justin explain it all to them? How could he prove to them that he loved them? How would they ever again know with certainty?

He collapsed to his knees, knelt there, back bent, forehead on the floor, and wept. Eventually his crying ceased and he levered himself up, his body feeling like lead. He picked up his rucksack, looked just once and slowly around the room at the final signs of his presence that he had left – the helpless, hopeless scribbled words – and left, carefully closing the bedroom door.

Downstairs he left his Yale key on the window sill by the door: he could not bear to keep the means to re-enter his home knowing it was out of bounds. Closing the door almost tenderly, he walked down the garden path, threw his rucksack into the back of the campervan, and drove away, his face wet with silent tears.

Driving in a daze, he knew he was heading north – knew, without thinking it out, that he had to isolate himself in a wilderness. He was drawn to desolation. His driving and perceptions were automatic: he turned corners and changed gears without realising it. Beating and repeating endlessly in his head were the words "I will never live with them again. I will never live with them again." They filled his consciousness for mile after mile, hour after hour.

He noticed bright lipstick smeared on his fingers; had brief, flashing images of Tom and Abi's pyjamas scattered on their beds, of them asleep with thumbs in their mouths, of Abi laughing on the swings in Ninian Park, of Tom's face grinning and smeared with chocolate. The images flared in his mind like matches in the darkness – they burned him and he jerked away, wincing at their clarity.

When he knew they would all be back from playgroup he stopped just over the Forth Bridge at a roadside phone box and telephoned home. Vicky answered. He poured out his terror to her in clumps of words knotted between bouts of weeping. He couldn't cope, did not know how to cope, could not face it. She listened, tried to calm him but she was resolute. He would learn to live with it, she said, he would see the kids regularly. He came to the end of his pile of coins and the call just ceased, his words amputated. He stood there in the red phone box with the black plastic receiver in his hand, the dial tone in his ear, traffic busy on the road, the sunshine indifferent. He placed the receiver back on the stand and slumped into the corner, his forehead on the cold glass pane. The cold glass and metal, solid, insentient, practical, mocked the swirling whirlpool of his emotions that filled this small, silent, containing space.

He opened the door, the breeze freshening his face which, though still wet with tears, felt strained dry, drawn taut over his bones. Back in the van he started the engine and drove off. He was quieter now, subdued by exhaustion. In the late afternoon he decided he would motor on to the far north and stop for food and a map in Dingwall. It would be the furthest north he had ever been. He had been reading John Prebble's *The Highland Clearances*, had brought it with him in his rucksack. He would find a place mentioned in it – Croick churchyard – near where whole villages and hamlets had been cleared out, the tenants evicted and their homes burned down. It would be the appropriate place for him.

At Dingwall he bought some bread, butter, tea, coffee, cheese, bacon, cereal, milk, soup – and a bottle of his favourite Laphroaig whisky. He filled up with petrol, sat morosely drinking a coffee in a drab roadside café for half an hour, watched people going about their usual business, unaware of him, and set off again. He drove up the Cromarty Firth, past Invergordon with its oil rigs, picturesque Tain, and turned off the main road, going west, at Ardgay.

Slowly he drove up Strathcarron on the narrow road with passing places. The valley was wide and shallow, with conifer plantations, rising to moors and low hills to north and south. It was now around 7pm; he was tired and hungry. He looked for a place to park the van overnight and found a spot on the north bank of the River Carron next to where a stream joined the main river, a grassy pull-in edged with gorse and a few large boulders. He manoeuvred the van so he had a view along the river, and turned off the engine. There was complete silence.

Looking around, the sky was grey and darkening off to the west. It looked like rain. He could see a couple of cottages along the edge of the plantations. There were no people in view. He got out, stretched and walked a little along the riverbank. The water was beautifully clear, rushing noisily over the rocks, with still pools left under the overhang of the bank.

Back in the van, he boiled a kettle and made a mug of tea, ate a cheese sandwich, tidied up. Darkness settled over the valley, with no sunset. The calm demise of the day suited his mood: he was spent, all emotion drained from him. He had no plan other than to stay here for a few days, endure what had to be endured, and then return. He opened the whisky and poured himself a large one, sipped it frequently but not desperately, savouring the burn in his throat, the peaty, smoky tang. A huge sadness enveloped him like the night as he pictured Abi and Tom going to bed, Tom falling asleep as Justin read a story to them. Would Abi wonder where her father was, what was happening to him, why he was no longer there? Was she sad, upset? Was Tom too young to understand? Maybe this was his only consolation. He forced himself to endure his imagining, refusing to switch his mind elsewhere. He deserved this punishment. The whisky did not dull his suffering. He finished his glass, reorganised the van into a bed, peed by the river, got into his sleeping bag and subsided into eventual sleep.

Next morning was sunny and still. The business of ablutions and breakfast soothed him. Over his third coffee he read in *The Highland Clearances* a section that dealt with Strathcarron, where he was camped. As the book began a detailed report of what happened in the 1830s, Jack decided to visit the exact place and follow the events on the ground where they had actually occurred. He packed up the bed, rolled up his sleeping bag and put it away in the cupboard, washed and dried the pots. He had a purpose for the day, a schedule, practicalities that would give him a focus, take him out of his own misery.

He drove up the glen to where the Black Water joined the Carron, parked the van and walked up a track through the Amat Forest, crossed a bridge over the Carron and down to where the Calvie joined the Carron. He sat in the sun, with his back against a rock, at the very place where a crowd of village women had gathered and lit a peat fire. The women had smiled and called out to the sheriff's officers for the writs and when the papers were handed to them they threw them on the fire. But two years later the main tenants were tricked by the factor James Gillander and, by the spring of 1845, all

41

the cottages at Glencalvie had been emptied except for one where an 82-year-old pensioner, Hugh Ross, who had served in India, was dying.

He walked up the glen by the clear, fast-running River Calvie. The only sounds were the river, the calls of curlews up on the hills and the bleating of lambs. The morning was still warm, soft and windless. Along the river he soon came to the remains of the crofters' cottages. If he hadn't been looking for them he would not have recognised them. All that was left of their walls were mounds, about eighteen inches high, covered in turf – the doorways gaps in the rectangular shapes. He walked slowly among them: these once were homes, with laughter and arguments, business and bitterness – all the complexities of people living together. And in such a beautiful place. Long stretches of wire fencing, high to keep the deer out and the sheep in, had replaced the fallen field-walls. Jack looked around. His own private misery was self-imposed, he thought. His dispossession had been caused by his own self-indulgence. The people whose misery he was reading about had done nothing wrong and were the helpless victims of others' greedy exploitation and selfishness. Their circumstances put his into perspective.

Jack turned and walked back up to the small churchyard of Croick. This had been the only refuge for the evicted tenants, a little walled enclosure sheltered by a few bent trees. Although it was May, the weather had been wet and cold. Behind the church a long kind of booth was erected, the roof formed of tarpaulin stretched over poles, the sides closed in with horsecloths, rugs, blankets and plaids.

His book said that while the Glencalvie people were there they had scratched their names and brief messages on the diamond-paned windows of the church. Although they spoke Gaelic they had written in English as if acknowledging that their own tongue would pass away with them and would not be understood in future times.

He looked for the place and there, under a second, protective pane of glass, he read: *"Glencalvie people was in the church here May 24 1845... Glencalvie people the wicked generation... John Ross shepherd... Glencalvie people was here... Amy Ross Glencalvie is a wilderness blow ship them to the colony... the Glencalvie Rosses..."*

"The wicked generation" – so brainwashed by the church that they had concluded it was their own fault. He went into the small, unlocked church. It was bare, simple, clean, built by Thomas Telford. There was a smell of damp. He signed the visitors' book, wondering if Abi or Tom would ever come here and see his signature, know anything of why he had come.

Outside again, chilled by the church, he relaxed into the warmth of the sun. His own misery was all-enveloping and yet, in the context of this tiny community's tragedy – repeated all over the west and north of Scotland – his was not a tragedy but an utter foolishness brought on by a lack of steadfastness and decency. The tragedy was for Abi and Tom, deprived of growing up in a stable and happy family. His suffering, though real, was born of weakness. Here he was, alone in a desolate place – though the sun was shining from a blue sky – making his despair into a kind of performance, albeit with no audience but himself.

Then he realised he was hungry. His appetite never let him down – it was a gift, a benison. No matter how high or low his mood – ecstasy or misery – his stomach could be guaranteed to recall him to reality. He walked back to the van, drove down Strathcarron and found a place to park near Wester Greenyards, left the sliding door open, heated a tin of soup – Cock-a-leekie, of course – and made a Scots Cheddar cheese sandwich.

Somehow he had begun to sense what he was up here for in this far northern glen: he knew he would survive. But in order to survive he had to sink as deeply as possible into the fullest experience of his misery and loneliness. He must not avoid it either by being with other people or by drinking whisky. He had to descend the well of darkness in order to ascend into the light again. When he could cry and agonise no more, he would emerge stronger, able to cope.

At the end of the week he took the road back to Swansea, to the children he loved and the new life he must make around them for their sake. He realised that what he had never fully valued, he had now lost irretrievably. He could only endeavour to minimise the harm he had already done to them. He would keep faith with them, better late than never, better in briefer, intense times than in the sameness of everyday. But even as he outlined his plan for himself he shuddered at its implausibility. It was an end to normality.

*

Jack gives a deep sigh. *Is that what the rest of the week will be – painful memories but for no greater understanding?*

But how to fit that time – and the other memories he had waiting – into the pattern, if there was one, of his life? An epiphany was what he craved, a revelation – like a grouse bursting out from beneath his feet in a whirl of wings and a clattering call. Then, satisfied, in a few days, in some way not yet decided, he would make an end of it all, but properly this time.

That's what I call progress. Maturity for me is going round in a bloody circle. Amazing though it is, my kids have forgiven me, they've moved on. Have I? My guilt circles ceaselessly with the oxygen into my brain, no escape from it. I will die with it. Well, so be it! That's me.

Jack had always been astonished when people said they had no regrets. It wasn't a matter of living virtuously. No, they must hold to this fashionable theory that feelings of guilt were harmful. Jack, however, believed in guilt: guilt unbolted the shutters so he could gaze through the window into his... he wouldn't call it soul... into his conscience, consciousness, the microchips of his brain. Guilt was a path to self-discovery. It accurately defined the inadequate and, yes, the bad, in him. It confirmed he was human – a backhanded compliment if ever there was one. Because he did not deserve forgiveness, he did not seek it. Accepting his own guilt simultaneously made it easier to live with himself and to relinquish living.

He takes a last swig of water and repacks his rucksack, flexes his fingers – it was becoming a bit of a nervous habit. *Jesus! Is this what it's going to be like for the rest of the walk – just more questions? I need some answers.* It was as if he had set himself an exam that he was predestined to fail. *But I sort of knew that from the start.* He laughs out loud. *Perhaps being an atheist is just a way of avoiding Judgement Day. Balls to it!*

How had Abi and Tom been able to forgive him? Because he had tried? Because he had finally kept faith – visited them every other weekend? Now grown up, we have good times together. How eagerly they assure me they value my advice and identify traits and interests they have inherited from me. They are kindly, loving people – in spite of me, I suppose.

The following year had been full of upheaval, he remembered. Laura had told him to leave. He had been like a moth to a flame, he had soon realised. Vicky and Justin had moved from Swansea to Manchester and Jack had visited his children by train every other weekend, hiring a car and taking them to parks or swimming or ice-skating. Then Vicky had sent him a letter – he still had it in a folder somewhere – saying that she and Justin were not able to establish a new family because of his visits and limiting him to every three weeks. He remembered his ferocious and powerless anger. Then they had moved again, to Newcastle, too far for him to travel regularly for a weekend. So he had found a job in Newcastle and moved there. How Justin and Vicky must have resented that, how they must have been surprised, not expecting such a move from such a self-centred man. He took Abi and Tom on holidays, too, with his campervan: to Galloway and here to North Wales, taking them to the same beaches he had played on as a child. Now they have growing families and he has helped them with cash. *Buying their affection?* He has never thought of it that way before. *That's horrible!*

Yes, I'm going to give myself seven out of ten. Perhaps I did manage to cope with something alone, perhaps Strathcarron was my equivalent to Tom's going to Spain. My children have been my only sustained fidelity. Apart from Branwen, but that had surprised even me. How real had that been? Or is it really only the foolish fiction of a doddering pensioner?

He feared again what it meant about him: that he seemed to empathise with characters in a book or a film more than with real people: the Glencalvie folk. It was easier to immerse himself into fictional or historical characters than living people – probably because he had no obligations to them, because he moved on to another book, leaving no trail of disappointment or anguish. Had he turned Branwen into a fiction?

Where have I read that the only lasting passion is an impossible one? Branwen – who has also walked these shores with me. Does she have an image of me here now? Or has she just deleted my text and also deleted me from her mind? Pointless to speculate. Time for episode two: the re-entry of Branwen into my life after Kathy's death, the pivot around which the rest of my life will turn. Though I didn't know it then.

★

Five years had passed since Kathy's death. Jack and Megan had constructed a life together. "You just have to get on," she said. "Yes, I'm sad sometimes but that's how it is." Being an only child, friends had always been important to Megan but Jack now observed them take on a greater significance. She had a close circle of good friends to whom she was intensely loyal, taking on the role of listener to their several problems.

She loved school – all her friends were there – and she worked hard. The intelligence she had, she fully utilised. She was a grafter. She had a soft spot for naughty, mischievous boys. She played for the school at netball, hockey and badminton. With two of her friends she played rugby league. Jack never forgot the Saturday mornings he watched her playing in pouring rain on windy, exposed pitches against the tough girls of inner city teams. She didn't flinch or shirk and he loved her for that. Then suddenly she gave it up, maybe because she was afraid of getting hurt as she developed into a young woman. She never explained.

Megan terrified him when she expanded her friendship group and started going to nightclubs – her breakout, thought Jack, from all the virtuous expectations of her. He never slept before she returned, often in a taxi, from those outings to the city. Lying awake, he imagined the worst. Once she spoke knowledgeably about the morning-after pill. Would she have confided more to Kathy? Would she be able to talk to him in the way she would have talked to Kathy? Was it possible for a man to be both mother and father? How vulnerable she was, in spite of her intelligence, more needy of affection and love now her mother was gone. He had to trust her and trust that, together, they struck the right balance between letting her find her own way and keeping her safe. Jack was sure there were sides to her he did not know and she wouldn't want him to know. He knew that was all about growing up, the inevitable – and healthy – growing apart.

On the night before her A-level results came through Jack slept not a wink. He knew how crucial they were. He wept tears of joy for her when she won a good university place. It was far away but he loved that, too, as she set out to be independent.

He drove her there with a carload of stuff, helped her to sort her room, loved her eagerness and confidence but worried that it might not turn out as she thought. He remembered his own mother tearfully waving goodbye as he went off to university on the train, the first of his family ever to go. He understood her feelings. Sure enough, in two days, she phoned.

"I don't like the people here, they're all public school. I want to come home and start somewhere else next year."

But Jack didn't want her to give in. He persuaded her to stay and ask to be moved from her hall of residence. She found a house to share with compatible friends and the problem was over. He loved it when she sent him the drafts of her essays.

Now he was truly alone and the house was silent, empty of Megan's bustle and things, her bedroom no longer alternating between chaos and extreme tidiness. He began to think back over his life: there was much to apologise for. It seemed a bizarre idea at first. Those people he had hurt would have moved on – and literally: he had lost track of them. But Branwen, he knew about. Had he thanked her enough at the time for that desperate phone call he had made? She had given him a forgiveness he had needed. To her, above all, he owed an apology. Or was this just a pretext to see her again? Memories of their time together came unbidden to his mind and he savoured them. He still had friends in Swansea from the project and one had a holiday cottage to rent. He arranged to spend a long weekend there. Via the same circuitous route he had used before, he asked that Branwen send him her email address. She complied – which removed his first anxiety – and he explained his brief holiday arrangements. Could he meet her for dinner? Back came the email: "Yes," with the address of the restaurant she had chosen. 7pm. "Bring some family photos," she ended.

So Jack was early, waiting outside the restaurant, his hood

up in the rain. He was expecting her to walk towards him, knowing he would recognise her bearing and the shape of her legs. A taxi drew up, Branwen got out and turned to Jack who stepped towards her. He kissed her briefly on the cheek, felt her flinch, draw back, heard the car drive away, and then they were inside the restaurant.

They sat down at one of a line of tables, not very private, menus in their hands but looking at each other, unsure what to say. Jack didn't want to say anything, wanted to freeze-frame so he could just take her in. She had not aged, OK a few lines around her eyes, hair shorter now and expensively styled. Her smile the same, the full sensuous lips he remembered. She was still trim and lithe. Her clothes seemed classy, conservative, in subdued colours. She looked well-to-do. He was also looking for clues: what was she making of him? Was she already regretting her decision? Was she curious? Was she recalling the past?

"First thing," she said, "we're going halves. There's no such thing as a free meal."

She smiled at him. No obligations, she meant. He understood the ground rules she was laying down, prescribing the evening ahead. She was self-assured and decisive; she had become her own person.

Once the waitress had taken their order and the red wine had been brought and poured, Jack thanked her for her response to his phone call. She replied:

"When you rang, it was such a shock. And then you told me about Kathy's car crash and how you felt some kind of responsibility. I had no time to think. I'm a marriage guidance counsellor – you may smile – but all that suddenly disappeared. I just spoke instinctively."

"Even better. You said exactly the right thing."

He paused, sipped his wine and drew a deep breath: "The real reason I wanted to see you was to apologise for how I treated you all those years ago. What I did and how I did it was inexcusable. Laura was a huge mistake. I know I can't make amends but I never explained or apologised to you at the time."

It was her turn to pause. She looked directly into his eyes, as she always had done. "Jack, there is no need to apologise. It was long ago, a different world, it doesn't matter now."

Jack wanted to hold her hand, to stroke her face softly with the back of his fingers. She was smiling at him.

"We weren't together all that long, Jack, just a few months. But it was life-changing for me. It was hard, I won't deny it, at the time. I hated you and loved you. It took a long time to recover from. But I did and it helped me know myself better. If you hadn't gone away I wouldn't have married Hugh nor had my wonderful children."

She held no resentment towards him and he should have been pleased, released. But her picture of her happy marriage, her obvious success and prosperity, only emphasised how much he had lost – and all for the fantasy of Laura.

"So that's that," she said. "You've apologised and I've accepted. That's the end of it. Now let's see your photos of Abi and Tom."

He remembered how well she had played with them in the park, all her fun and humour. Sadness threatened to envelop him but he must make this evening a success. Perhaps it was the last time he would see her. So he took out the photos and Branwen studied them, said she could see traces of the young children she had known.

"And this is Megan," said Jack. "I am so proud of her."

"She has a strong face, Jack. She's lovely. All your children are lovely."

Then she took out her photos – of her three children when young and now as successful professionals. She would have been a good mother – sensible, loving, quite strict in some ways, a mother they could talk to and confide in. He was looking at the proof of her success.

"And here's Hugh and me on a cruise to celebrate our twenty-fifth wedding anniversary."

Jack took the photo: certainly an attractive couple, in their evening dress. He had to conceal his envy, his jealousy. She looked happy, content, quietly proud. Did he not have the generosity of spirit to accept that, to reciprocate her own generosity?

"You look very happy," he said.

"We are," she said.

They ate their meal and talked of what they had done and what had happened to them over the twenty-five intervening years: careers, travels, illnesses, their children's achievements. They did not stint on their wine and Jack several times felt Branwen examining his face. He wondered if, like him, she wanted to go over every contour, every feature and rediscover it, mark the changes of age. She held the wine glass in her long fingers, the light glinting through it, looking at him over the top of it, smiling. Softening, he thought, warming. He looked at her, knowing that all his physical longing for her was back. He gave a half smile, uncertain of what she was feeling.

"I remember," she said, "how your voice on the phone in the old days always sounded close to a smile or a laugh."

"That's what I think of Tom's," he said.

"Like father, like son."

He didn't order another bottle of wine. He walked her home, dallying the long walk along the dark streets, the rain holding off. She halted him before the end of her road. Did she fear her husband was watching out for her? He wanted to kiss her good night, but she stood a pace away, still in control.

"Thank you," he said, "thank you for coming. I didn't know what to expect. I've loved talking to you."

He was searching her face in the lamplight. She looked at him but he could read nothing there.

"Me, too," she said. "Good night."

Branwen turned away. Jack watched her go, hoping she would wave from the corner of her road. But she didn't. He took the long walk back. Young people were assembling around nightclub entrances. Their evenings were just beginning. He felt old and out of place, yet in all their youth and exuberance, did they have the rich complications of his feelings? His mind was brimful of emotions, snatches of their conversation. Wondering what she was thinking, what she was telling and not telling her husband. Even with the wine, it took him a long time to fall asleep.

Next day he went birdwatching as he had planned, walked the dunes and the coast path, listened to the male eiders' scandalous gossip as they rafted on the river estuary. His binoculars were on the birds but his mind was on Branwen. Why not? What had he to lose? Nothing ventured, nothing gained.

He phoned her from his mobile and, without preliminaries, asked if she would join him the next day to walk the estuary path. Sounding pleased but uncertain, she said she would ring back. For ten minutes Jack followed shelducks on the water, watched a tern fishing. His phone rang. Yes, she could come but not to the bird reserve. Jack should pick her up from her house after lunch and they would drive to a nearby village where there was a nice café. Disappointed yet elated, he agreed. From her house? That meant everything was in the open, her husband would have agreed.

Next day as he drew up in his hired car, he saw her watching for him from the window. She came out, shut the door behind her and got into the car. He wanted to give her a peck on the cheek but thought better of it. They drove and talked and she allowed him to buy her afternoon tea in the café. She kept the conversation on safe ground – more about children, reminiscing about their time on the project. She was as she had always been – chatty, pleasant, funny, optimistic. He was looking for signs that she was feeling some of what he was feeling – a great affection, wanting to hold her hand, yearning for a physical contact. Then the afternoon was over. He drove her back in time for her husband's return from work, double-parking the car outside her house. She leaned across and kissed him full on the lips, her eyes mischievous. Then she was gone, with a brief wave from her doorway.

He was stunned. What did that mean? Out of the blue, in the street, outside her home. It was a question he pondered on his long train journey home, wallowing in memories of their time together all those years ago. Her warmth, her softness, her vibrancy and sensuality, her sense of fun. What a fool he had been. He had thrown a pearl away.

*

He sighs deeply, lost in the memory. His legs and back have stiffened up.

All of it is over. Time to move on.

He stretches, bends, flexes his ankles and leaves the churchyard, carefully latching the gate behind him. Jack is feeling weary as he begins to slant up across Moel Ty-gwyn. *This is more of a penance than I bargained for, a lot of ups and downs today. I've had enough of climbing, and every climb means a descent and a descent means pain.* He passes yet another disused quarry, some white-painted cottages spaced out along a minor road, untidy yards full of stuff, not gentrified, and then the path heads between two low hills towards a plantation of trees. *Carnivorous? That's not the word – a meat-eating forest? What is the word?* Annoyed at his mistake, Jack tries variations. But where a stile leads into the forest, the trees have all been cut down, dead brushwood lying all around, slashed trunks. In the late afternoon light, his body tired, the place looks eerie. *Coniferous! That's it.* Jack's relieved his mind has retrieved the correct word.

He studies his map and the guidebook. Yes, the dotted path goes through a coniferous green plantation. The book gives details about the track bearing left with branches barring other directions and then moving on to a heather-covered glade. But what now with the trees cut? He crosses the stile with some apprehension. He doesn't want to get lost at the end of this long day. He follows what appears to be a cleared way winding through the cropped trees, enters a copse of uncut trees and then emerges into a field. He is relieved. Perhaps he likes to pore over maps and guidebooks because they show distinct routes, with markers – cairns or white-topped posts – and destinations, connecting point to point. The direction of his own life has been without markers, changing direction randomly and only now a final destination appearing. Across the field he reaches a track, then a lane and finally a signed footpath leads steeply down to the small town of Nefyn. It is the final punishment for his knees. He hopes there is a bath and not just a shower: his leg muscles need a long hot soak.

3. WALK, DAY THREE

Jack wakes to what he thinks is the ticking of the radiator as the central heating turns on. Then he realises it is dripping rain. He deliberately did not look at weather forecasts, preferring the unexpected to the predicted, but always carrying a proper range of clothing. Looking out of the hotel window he can see the pavement shining wet.

The golfers he saw in the bar last evening are already down for breakfast, in their red and yellow or orange and grey diamond sweaters.

"I didn't get a wink of sleep last night," says one. "It's tough being top of the leader board."

Groans and laughs.

Today's walk is entirely along the shore, visiting beaches that are full of memories for Jack. At least there will be no more hill-climbing. As he goes down the hotel steps, gingerly to get his knees gradually into gear, it is starting to drizzle. In his pack is a small wooden octahedron – the platonic shape symbolising air, its eight equilateral triangles swivelling freely when his fingers hold the opposite vertices. Well, the air is wet and looks as if it is going to get wetter. He zips up his waterproof jacket.

A runner passes him on the cliff path above Nefyn beach, grey hair plastered to his head, blue vest soaked with sweat and rain. It is beginning to rain hard now. At a wooden bench he sits down and begins the laborious task of putting on his waterproof over-trousers. Even though he can unzip them up to the knee he finds his arms and shoulders straining to fit them over his boots. The simplest tasks seem more difficult

55

now. Once past Penrhyn Nefyn he is on the exposed cliff top along the long bay of Porth Dinllaen. The wind has risen and the rain has intensified. He velcroes his hood tight around his neck, puts his head down and plods on. This is where he wants to savour his memories but the weather overrides them. He just wants to get to the pub at the hamlet on the beach – hoping that it's open for hot coffee.

The path turns inland and joins the uphill drive to the golf clubhouse. Its car park is full of cars but the fairways are empty, rain driving across them in great swathes, wind whipping the flags. He plods on across the golf course, totally exposed, until the narrow track turns down into the shelter of a gully that leads to the shore and the straggle of cottages. The pub door is open and he goes in, conscious of dripping water across the floor.

Behind the bar a plump man is sitting at a laptop. Without turning round, he says:

"What can I get you?"

There's no decaffeinated coffee but the mug of hot chocolate is perfect, in a dark corner of the pub, rain streaming down the window. He looks out across the bleak, empty beach, the refracted masts of yachts tossing on the sea. Weird how this tiny place has collated so many of his memories, threading the generations of his family.

Out of the corner of his eye he sees, in the kitchen behind the bar, a young woman in a red rugby jersey: an instant picture of Kathy wearing her favourite red Welsh rugby jersey, the sway of her full skirt as she moved, so quick and deft, doing ordinary things about the house, light-footed in her black pumps.

More than sixty years ago he was here for the first time – part of the family cavalcade that took the same path he had today but burdened with all the paraphernalia of a family outing shared among grandfather, parents, brothers and sister: travel rugs, beach towels, picnic baskets crammed with egg mayonnaise sliced white bread sandwiches, folding chairs, games gear. His grandfather, bowlegged with walking stick, long khaki shorts, Hawaiian shirt and straw hat; his father, overweight, struggling to walk with the arterial sclerosis in his legs but determined to get there; his mother in her flowered skirt and sandals; his younger siblings with buckets and spades and Frisbees and fishing nets. What an operation it now seems. He can remember irritations but no sadness; they were happy times, uncomplicated for him. All he had wanted to do was fit on his black flippers and snorkel and swim out into the ice-cold water of the bay, grazing his chest on the sand as he found razor-shells or swimming out to grasp the ropes of the yachts' buoys. Always when he returned his mother admonished him for swimming too far out and his father praised him.

Then after lunch he would drift away to walk along the rough shoreline path across the rocks and round to the next bay where there was a hidden beach and a lifeboat station, and then further to the very end of the promontory where he would sit and watch the waves breaking on the black rocks, no other person in sight. *Even then I was happier alone – but with family not far away. The pretend solitary. Plastic.* Late in the afternoon they would all trudge back, worn out by exercise and sun, sand in sandals and hair, complaining about having too much to carry and not being allowed to scurry up the shortcut of the steep cliff path.

Years later he brought Abi and Tom here, but with less baggage. He watched them play, went with them into the sea, built sandcastles with them, with channels to the sea. They watched the incoming tide slowly collapse the towers and walls, carefully placed pebbles falling into the sand. Later still he came with Kathy and Megan, the same pattern of activities, the same simple pleasures, the same happiness.

All he can remember is the happiness, not the fracturing that came before and afterwards, the broken pieces. He had walked here with Branwen too, after their reunion. And last year he brought his grandsons to repeat the rituals. Five generations had come here. That was where the sadness came in: not being all together, no embodied continuity.

The rain has not lessened, there are white horses on the waves. But he has to go, miles to walk to his next bed. Then the publican, once more leaning over his laptop, announces:

"The Norwegian weather forecast promises gales and even snow. They're usually more reliable than our Met. Office."

With that cheering news, Jack prepares himself for the fray and sets off. Head down, glasses covered with rain, leaning into the battering wind from the sea, the warmth of the hot chocolate soon dissipates. He crosses the golf course to a small bridge, the wood wet and slippy, over a stream that falls into a little bay, disfigured by a pipeline that dissects it. Waves crash into the rocks, white water seething. This is a long stretch of cliff-walking, crossing stiles into hedgerowed fields, occasional footpath signposts, no cottages or farms in sight. Huge curves of waves cream in along the coast, the grey sea merging into mist.

He is feeling chilled now in spite of his constant walking. He feels wet patches on his knees and shoulders. He wonders if his rucksack is still waterproof: his camera is in there. Then the battering of the rain on his hood diminishes to a light patter. In a few minutes it has stopped. Grey clouds are still racing away over him but out at sea it is clearer, a band of white sky on the horizon. There are even patches of blue sky and the occasional patch of sunlight. He unzips his hood and water trickles down his arm. His mind begins to function again.

His stomach too is communicating. He hasn't felt like sitting down in the pouring rain to open his rucksack and eat his sandwiches. Now he feels hungry and it is late. He will eat at Towyn beach. He knows it well as Tudweiliog beach, and he will find shelter from the wind behind the high rocks. Within an hour he is descending the familiar farm track, bending round to the perfect bay, the sand bare. He remembers that, up to the right, there are rocks which create a sheltered spot when the wind is blowing from the sea – how often had the family settled there when he was a child? Feeling like a despoiler, he walks out onto the unmarked sand. Never before has he been the sole person on this beach. In the shelter of the rocks he labours off his rucksack, finds a relatively flat place on the sharp, black, volcanic rock and unfolds his seat mat – another token of his age. He pours himself a coffee from the flask then looks back at the trail of his footprints, the indentations, the tread patterns of his boots, the low ridges of displaced sand. A lifetime ago his bare feet scampered across here, churning the sand, as he raced to the waves: what is left of that younger self? In what sense is he the same being?

How his young grandsons pealed with laughter at the name Tud – willy – og. His father had begun the narrative, coming with his mother in the 1920s to stay at a nearby farm, each night in bed watching mice feet running across the ceiling sheet above his head. Jack's father had never known his own father who had died when he was still a tiny baby. Jack's father had told his own mother – Jack's grandmother, who had told him this story – at the age of ten that one day he would bring his family, a real family, to this beach. He did: bringing her and his wife, Jack and his brothers and sister and their Springer Spaniel, Peg. Jack even remembered him embracing his mother as they stood at the end of the track where it joined the beach. It had been one of the very few times he had seen his father's eyes full of tears. They had played cricket here, his mother fielding and batting, and football. His father had taken them crabbing in the same pools he had crabbed in when he was a child. Jack himself had preferred swimming out and around the rocky outcrops, in defiance of his mother who told him never to go out of sight, clambering out gingerly on the sharp, rocky edges, watching the tide swill in between the rocks. Much later Jack continued the story when he brought Abi and Tom, and later still Kathy and Megan, and after that Branwen.

Now he is here alone. All those family strands are broken, the edges frayed, the pattern distorted. He suddenly understands why one of his favourite compositions for photography is a line of old slanting fence posts, all askew, mossed or lichened, no longer wired together, stretching into water, refracted and then disappearing below the water surface. That scene reflects his own life of disconnected directions, of perimeters now meaningless, of intentions confounded.

He remembers his mother, sitting on a low canvas chair on the purple travel rug – now an heirloom in Tom's family travel kit. She is leaning back, eyes closed, dozing, wearing her fawn cardigan for there is usually a breeze at Tudweiliog. How seldom he saw her relaxed. Her eyes will be closed for a few moments only as she opens them to immediately check the safety of her brood. She will insist on suncream, will towel his younger brothers when they come shivering from too long in the sea, she will supervise the distribution of sandwiches. Everything revolves around her. She was brimful of her role and responsibilities, brimful too of her happiness in her healthy, growing children.

So it is time for his next contemplation.

*

In the two weeks before one of his weekend visits, his mother had fallen over three times, stepping up a kerb. The last time, the right side of her face was bruised the colour of an aubergine and her nose was cut. She had fallen directly on her face again, yet again no bones were broken; they must be incredibly strong. She put the fall down to her bifocals or the soles of her shoes that slip. Jack knew it was because she no longer lifted her feet high enough when she walked. She would not accept this, not knowing how slowly she now shuffled along the pavement whereas only three months ago she walked almost normally. She had refused to use a stick though she was ninety-one.

When Jack came down for breakfast, his mother was sitting at the kitchen table in her dressing gown.

"I'm in a mess," she said, "My glasses – I've looked everywhere for them and can't find them."

Her pale eyes were watery, red-rimmed, bagged underneath. She looked exhausted.

"I want to be dead," she said. "I have nothing to plan for. It's ridiculous us living so long, with our faculties going. I'm ready to go sometimes." She sighed. "When I sit down, I don't want to get up again. But you've got to make the most of a bad job."

Jack hesitantly put his arms around her skeletal body and kissed her forehead. He made her fresh tea and toast and went to search for her glasses, which he found in her bedclothes. He gave them to her and cuddled her again. She put her arm around his waist – for the first time ever that he could remember.

"I'm glad you're here," she said. "You know," and her face began to break up, her mouth to waver, "I miss your dad now more than I ever did. I used to be able to walk along the promenade but now I can't."

His father had died of a heart attack more than thirty years ago and since then she had lived alone. After all the years of her bravely reconstructed life, she needed his father again. No longer self-sufficient, her world was narrowing because

61

she could no longer walk or drive or go out in the evening; she was confined. After a lifetime of perfect health she had to adapt to weaknesses: bits of broken tooth that emerged from her gums, an arthritic thumb, flutterings of her heart with its two leaking valves, dry eyes (drops six times a day, each application timed to the minute in her diary so she didn't forget), blood pressure pills, unsightly skin sagging on her arms (so she now only wears long-sleeved blouses), increasing deafness, aching bunions. Her constant fears were of losing her eyesight, having a disabling stroke, of the future, of the burdens of the big house she now wished she had left, of all her money going in nursing home fees.

"I want to ask the doctor if people like me – with my kind of heart problem – are more likely to have a stroke that kills them outright or one that disables them."

But he won't be able to predict, Jack thinks.

"I'd have the whole house pointed but I'll die in a couple of years. There's nothing good about growing old, Jack. You just stop being able to do things and wanting to do things. Whatever you want to do, do it now, Jack, before it's too late."

She sipped her tea and left the crusts of her toast.

"I'm fed up, Jack. I'm sick and daft. There's no point in living like this. I'm not behaving properly sometimes. Am I going funny? Yesterday I got up and overbalanced and fell back on the bed, only on the soft mattress, but I wonder if I'll hit my head. The other night I fell out of bed again. It took me ages to get back in. I'll have to tie myself in."

Jack imagined her in the dark, on her knees, no glasses, unable to see, in her long nightie, scrabbling to haul herself up. No one there to help. She was so brave, determined and strong. She was adamant she would not go into a care home. She had enough money but this was her legacy to her children.

"I'm not a person who needs a lot of company. I'm self-sufficient. I don't go into cafés and socialise."

Jack worried at what went on in her head: most days alone and speaking to no one, in the silence of her deafness, in the confusion of her mind. She had let pans boil dry because she had forgotten them, often didn't know what day it was until she looked at her Daily Telegraph. Until he bought her a 24-hour digital clock, she often didn't know, on awakening from an all-night sleep in her easy chair in the lounge, whether it was seven in the morning or seven at night ("I'll be able to tell in the winter"). She forgot the instructions about how to put on and put off her new electric fire – which they selected together and which she now loved ("it makes everything so cosy, and the flames go quite high. I wonder why the pieces of coal don't burn"). Yesterday, she told Jack, she awoke at ten to one, at lunchtime, and she had been sitting in the tub chair in the bay window where she watched the sparse life go by in her street – she knew when the headmaster went out and returned, when his sons were home, when the nurse opposite was on different shifts – and she was still in her nightdress and hadn't had any breakfast so she was hungry.

Her kitchen – which had always been the centre of her world – was a mess. Had she been conscious of it, she would have been horrified. When he had arrived he had found a meal from three days ago still in the oven, now green with mould. There was green mould on the bread in the breadbin, a bag of rotting bananas in the corner so that when Jack had lifted it up to put in the bin a host of flies lifted off it.

She had been a humble woman, but proud too of what she had achieved. When they had discussed carers coming in to make sure she ate properly and took her medication she had said angrily:

"Stop thinking about me all the time. There are too many people getting involved in my life. People think you're gormless at my age. They won't let you do anything. They want to take over too much. They should leave me alone. I'm capable of doing things."

But she wasn't. She could no longer cook or even clean her dishes: she wasn't strong enough to scrub or even hold her small brown teapot in one hand. Yet she wheeled her wheelie bins down her path.

As she had rapidly grown more frail over the last eighteen months, Jack had wanted her to go into a residential home. Her deafness had become more intense, her eyesight failed, she walked in the house with a Zimmer, she was too weak to leave the house on her own. He had shown her round a home. Her conclusion: "There's one word that sums up that place, Jack – institutional. It's starchy."

So instead, after long persuasion, she had agreed to carers coming three times a day, whom she appreciated and resented in equal proportions.

"There's too many strangers coming into my house," she complained.

Her fatal fall, and how she dealt with it, told her story as well as anything else. What happened during the night they could only later piece together from his nephew's story, and from knowing her routine. Normally she was still in bed when the carers came at about nine o'clock. But she must have felt invigorated by having something to look forward to, an outing with some of her family – or perhaps she was just confused about time. They knew she got up and dressed herself, lacing up her favourite white shoes. Then, as she was about to get into her stairlift chair – maybe she had switched the landing light on – something had happened in her head or heart, some attack or other, or she had lost her footing and slipped. She had tumbled down the six steps to the landing and cracked her head on the steel stairlift rail. It was a fearful crack and she must have been knocked out. She must first of all have tried to crawl back up the stairs to her bedroom because Jack had noticed the footplate of the chair was raised, as it never was, as she tried to manoeuvre past. This had proved impossible and she had turned and somehow made her way downstairs, the stairlift still at the top because she could not climb into it, blood all the way down the stairs. Somehow she had prised herself up when she got down and hobbled past two telephones to sit in her easy chair in the lounge and wait for the carer to come. It would have been cold in the middle of the December night with no heating on.

When the carer arrived and found her she had immediately called the ambulance. Her daughter and grandson had come round. The paramedics got her into the ambulance and her grandson had said to her:

"These men will look after you, Grandma, and I'll come in the ambulance with you to the hospital."

Her immediate reply had been: "I can look after myself, thank you." She had added: "I'm brave, you know."

Jack had often told her how brave she was and she had always been dismissive: "You just get on and cope, Jack. There's nothing brave about it." Now he was so glad he had told her, maybe she had even listened. In the ambulance, in distress but still strong, she had allowed herself a compliment, had relaxed into a rare generosity about herself.

He had been told all this in a phone call from his nephew. She was now in hospital, unconscious, they had done a CT scan and she had had a massive haemorrhage. She had been placed on a side ward with morphine and oxygen so she could gently and painlessly slip away. She could have no more than half an hour to live, they had been told. There was no point in rushing over. Jack's immediate reaction, to his lasting shame, had been to agree. Then he had come to his senses and driven over. He thought of her in her chair after her fall. He could not rid himself of questions: had she been in pain? Conscious? Had she in some way understood this was her bravest moment, the zenith of managing on her own, of refusing help? He hoped so, how fervently he now hoped so – so that she would have a satisfaction with herself, would die with pride.

The hospital staff did not know his mother. She survived not half an hour but three days. At first as Jack watched her he was horrified: on her temple a piece of gauze did not conceal a massive bloody wound where she had cracked her head against the steel rail of her stairlift, her eyes were surrounded by deep purple blotches, the rest of her face was yellow and tinged with green. Her head was tipped back and her mouth open, already like a skull. But she breathed. She was fighting. Bruised and battered she was fighting against the withdrawal of life: her chest, in its pale blue patterned hospital nightgown, rose and fell steadily, her pulse beat in her neck, her breathing sometimes rasping.

Slowly his horror faded as he came to understand why he was there, why he would spend the nights with her, dozing on a reclining chair in her small, grey room. It was not just the last loyalty he owed her during the last, slow, struggling mile of her ninety-one-year marathon. He felt it was his last opportunity as her son to witness her strength of purpose, her tenacity, the independence that had seen her live alone for forty years. This vigil was a privilege. He was watching her last resistance, her last defiance of the ageing process she hated so vehemently. Jack realised, too, that she had successfully achieved her last two aims in life: to live to the end in her own home and to die cared for without expense in a hospital.

Jack was ashamed again that he had found it difficult to touch his mother in her hospital bed. Her skin was stained, her body skeletal. She was far beyond the mother who for sixty-five years had worried about him more than about herself: the practical, busy mother who had helped him with his maths homework, washed his rugby kit, interceded with his father when they had fearful rows. Far beyond the mother he wished to remember. But his nephews and their wives stroked her bloodstained hair and held her hand and talked to her. And just once he held her warm, smooth fingers and thought he felt a tightening of her fingers round his own – as the others did. For though she had been unconscious, with a large section of her brain dead, who knows what perceptions she still had? Had she recognised in the core reptilian part of her brain their familiar voices as, sitting around her bed, they reminisced and laughed and joked? If she had, it would have made her happy. Seeing her granddaughter-in-law pregnant and due to give birth in a month or so, she would have made some direct, blunt and unflinching observation about "out with the old and in with the new". On three occasions her eyes had half opened – grotesque and terrifying to Jack, that she might emerge into some kind of vegetative consciousness. It seemed to him she had been still struggling for a last communication.

Jack had wondered if there was a moment, at the very point of death, when there was a last perception? If there was, if there was for his mother, she would have experienced it alone, for no one was there when she drew her last breath at 9.15 two days later in the morning in a quiet corner of the hospital ward, about an hour before Jack was due to arrive. Had that been his last betrayal of her? Or had it been appropriate for her: to die alone as she lived for so long alone? To cope alone with the final challenge? That at least would be the solace he clung to.

And so Jack was glad that he had come to her bedside. He believed that if he had any strength himself he owed it to her. Only towards the very end had she allowed herself to need. He remembered driving away at the end of one of his fortnightly visits, waving to her. She was standing on the doorstep, waving back. He could not bear to look in his mirror to see her turn into her silent, empty house and close her door. Her last words to Jack were spoken on the phone:

"When are you coming to visit again?"

He would never forget them.

Jack went to the inquest: he didn't want the coroner or the pathologist or the attendant journalist to think that no one cared about this mother. It was an issue of respect. It was neither pointless nor just a formality. The occasion was like a final, formal signing-off of a life and it needed someone who loved her to witness it. It gave her memory a little final dignity.

After the inquest, Jack drove back to collect his mother's ashes from the undertakers and continued on to park on the promenade not far from what had been her home for thirty years. His mother's final wish, in a written note, was that her ashes be scattered in the sand-hills near where she had lived almost all her adult life. He locked the car and carried the tasteful maroon bag containing the plastic brown urn across the grass towards the beach. A pair of dog walkers and a pair of cyclists looked at him curiously. He was careful not to tread in dog shit. In his childhood this stretch of grass had been clean sand-hills. Coming to the beach he found it an expanse of brown grass, what sand there was, dirty with rubbishy shale. The tide was far out and he could see the thin, white line of breaking waves. The sky was a leaden grey. He followed a track into the few low remaining sand-hills. He found it an utterly depressing place, and somehow quintessentially his mother who was short on sentiment, imagination, grace and a sense of occasion. She was grimly practical and this was definitely a pragmatic choice as a final resting place.

He remembered the night his father had died, his body at the undertaker's, she had been sitting in front of the fire when she suddenly said quite simply that she no longer believed in God. She had never backtracked on that decision, not as she neared death herself, going to many funerals of her friends. She had been adamant: death was the end, there was nothing afterwards. She had never accepted the comfort of an afterlife

68

and possible reunions. Her resolution and self-sufficiency stayed until the end.

Jack found a small amphitheatre, or dell, of sand. There was no clean area anywhere. There were crushed cans of Strongbow and Carlsberg half trodden into the sand, plastic bottles and orange Sainsbury's plastic bags, the charred remains of driftwood fires. As he unscrewed the urn cap a couple of mongrel dogs wandered through on extended leads held by an overweight man and woman, both clutching clear plastic bags full of dog shit. He waited for them to pass. A strong wind was blowing from the sea. He took out about a dozen handfuls of his mother's white ashes and scattered them: the wind seized them and within yards and seconds they had disappeared, some into the sand, some blown as dust towards a stunted wind-blown clump of grey alders. He recapped the urn and placed it back in the bag. He noticed there were shards of broken green glass in the sand. It was a desolate place, shabby, prosaic, undistinguished. A plane droned overhead; the sea was grey, far out beyond the river channel. The ash dust was white on his fingers, ash under his nails. As he walked back to the car he saw a kite with streamers, flown by two boys who played among the brown marram grass. He walked to the copse of bare alders. A bright pink and white ice cream van drove by, its jingle playing.

He went back to her house. Already it too was dead although the evidence of her life was still there: the family photos on the piano, the old sheets with which she covered her cheap plastic conservatory chairs to protect them from the sun, the kitchen surfaces with her pill packets and eye drops, age-old letters from the Civic Society and Labour Party and Marine Park Bowling Club, the orange melamine surface peeling from her kitchen cupboard doors as it had for years.

It was a silent house. But it always had been, even before she had gone deaf. His mother had never listened to the radio or to music. She was unrelentingly on her own. Jack thought of her solitude that must have sometimes been loneliness. She never complained about her lot – except about the process of ageing. Upstairs the single bed in which she slept was neat and bright with the yellow, green and blue duvet. On her bedside table was an old-fashioned alarm clock, her spray to alleviate her lonely night-time heart fibrillations, and her Age Concern Cold Alert temperature gauge. Now that he had himself experienced some of the heart fibrillation she experienced Jack knew how terrified she must have been sometimes – alone at night with a pounding heart and sometimes the agony of cramp too. This was why he would always remember his mother as brave.

Four pairs of shoes were lined up by the wardrobe, each with their toes stuffed with newspaper: thriftiness was engrained in her.

The only visible signs of sentiment were the photographs on her dressing table, all black and white and in modest frames: her mother, soft-haired, has a gentle smile and wears a string of pearls; her father, suited and presidential, white-haired and with a confident smile – but his photo is discoloured with small blotches of damp; and her husband, Jack's father, who looks out with a direct gaze from beneath his high forehead, his arms folded, with his familiar, sardonic smile.

There was one other photograph – on its own, on the wall to one side of the bed. It was modestly sized and framed, of her at the age of five. It was a studio portrait, sepia-tinted. Her hair was fine, like her mother's, and she wore a wispy drape of voile across her bare shoulders. From a face half-turned towards the camera she looked at Jack directly but with a shyness. Jack looked back at her, his mother as a child, eighty-six years ago, in 1922, daughter of a baker in the Rossendale valley, seeking some signs of the strong qualities she had developed. In the photo he saw a fragility, a gentle delicateness that was not just the photographer's artfulness. There was a reticence but also an intensity in her eyes – as if she was eager for the sensitive fullness of life but was also in retreat from its boisterous vitality.

She hadn't made it easy for them – in many ways she kept life at bay, was never demonstrative, kept friends and neighbours at least one remove away. She was stubborn and often ungrateful. And Jack could never talk to her about his emotional life. She would have told him not to be silly. But by her life she taught her children to cope and to be independent. She kept her finances immaculately, sorted the bottles and cardboard for the recycling bins, forbade him to drink Advocaat because it was a woman's drink. In the hall was her leopard-skin hat on the hatstand, and her green coat. She never failed to put on her 'lippie' and comb her hair in front of the mirror before she went out.

She never demanded of him, thought Jack, never made him feel guilty. Only in the last nine months had she needed him, not liking to be left. She wanted him to lead his own life but he should have been bigger than just to accept that. He should have visited more often. Some of her weekends and evenings must have been so tedious and meaningless, which is why she had slept so much – not just tiredness but boredom, an escape.

Jack shut the front door, made sure he heard the Yale click into place. The final affront was the dark green patch of moss, insolent in the middle of her front lawn. That lawn had never been good enough for her.

★

He has one more ritual to face. From his rucksack he takes his wallet and from that wallet he unfolds a piece of typewritten paper. It is the obituary his mother wrote for herself, that she wanted read out at her funeral. He reads it again.

71

Her main interest in life was caring for her family and it was to this end that she gave all her love and devotion to her husband and her children. It was a great loss when her husband passed away at the age of fifty-five, but she rallied her mental and physical strength and she bravely faced widowhood.

Almost immediately after her husband's death she was appointed Justice of the Peace and sat on the bench for eighteen years serving on the Criminal, Family and Licensing Benches. This important and interesting work filled in much of her spare time and she also undertook a few hours' clerical work in a local office. Eventually grandchildren came along and she took a keen interest in their progress and development and Megan, Abi and Tom loved to hear their grandmother's stories of past times when she was younger.

She was a long-standing member and worker for the Civic Society and also Art Society. She was an enthusiastic member and untiring helper of the Townswomen's Guild for over thirty-five years, holding positions of Section Chairman, Secretary and President in turn, and was also an enthusiastic member of their choir.

Many years ago she was a founder member of the local Old People's Welfare Committee, which eventually became Age Concern. She was also a Governor of a Junior School for a short time later, which she was sorry to have to leave because of a change of structure.

At the age of seventy she began to play Crown Green Bowls and thoroughly enjoyed this sport and its competitiveness in the women's senior team, at the Bowling Club.

Despite filling her life with these different interests after the death of her husband, her family came first and foremost and she was always there to help and support them in every way she could – and she had the love and devotion of all of them in return.

Hymns for the church and crematorium:
Angel Voices Ever Singing
The Day Thou Gavest Lord is Ended
For the Beauty of the Earth

Jack had tried to imagine her writing this on her old portable typewriter, sitting alone at the dining room table, pondering. It could only have been some need for self-justification that impelled her to write this, some fear that the people she loved most did not appreciate how she had coped and what she had accomplished. She would never intend it as such, but what an accusation was implied. Had he not told her often enough how much he admired her? Had she felt her reconstruction of her life had been taken for granted, not understood? And yet he knew she was not someone who encouraged such compliments and certainly did not seek them out. She was not good at being grateful or accepting gifts. But what he found hardest to read were her final words: *she had the love and devotion of all of them in return*. Because the real core of her life had been her family, had she needed to blind herself to the truth? Was it something she could not deal with – that his love had been patchy and ungenerous?

And what of Jack himself? How often he had tried to draw up a balance sheet. He had told her he wanted her to come and live in the cottage next door to him when it came up for sale. "You all have your own lives," she had replied. "I won't live with any of my children. Old people bring problems into families." He had arranged for meals to be brought in, bought her a microwave (which she never learned to work), arranged for carers, filled in her income tax forms and managed her finances, took her away for day trips and weekends to the Lake District, had her over for Christmas, took his own children and grandchildren to visit her, planned a huge ninetieth birthday party for her to which her family travelled from New Zealand

and Canada and the USA, visited her every other weekend, made a photomontage of her sitting in her lounge, compiled a life story for her with old and present photographs.

Yes, he could give himself a pat on the back for those things. But he had not empathised sufficiently – not understood her need, her being unwell alone, her long, tedious days. He had not been with her at her final fall or at her death. One thing he knew she had been grateful for was something as painful to him as her auto-obituary.

"I want you all to have a photo of me when I'm gone," she had said to him, her eyes watering and her face breaking up a little. "But I don't know which one."

Jack told her he had several already. "Do you really think we won't remember you, Mum?"

So he had taken some portraits of her and she had chosen one she really liked – as he did. It was an honest picture: her neck was wrinkled, the rims of her eyes were red, her eyes watery. But her smile was gentle, the set of her face was strong and there was colour to her skin, she had had her grey hair done and she wore large pearl earrings, her white blouse had a delicate lace collar. She was looking directly at them. Jack had framed three copies and given them to Megan, Abi and Tom.

Jack's mother had never spoken of the fear of dying, only of having a disabling stroke. But Jack understood she was afraid of not being any longer in her children's and grandchildren's lives, of being nothing. That awful blank – especially as she does not believe in the afterlife and has rejected that comfort and compensation – that end of existence, is what now moves her.

Now it is Jack's turn to have these thoughts, concluding that once his grandchildren have died no one would be left who knew him or had been with him. Then it is that we finally die – remaining only as a fading photo on the piano top. It is brutal, but that's how it is. That's why monuments are built or battles fought, stamp collections and rings made into family heirlooms, bits of attempted biography written.

He puts the obituary back into his wallet. How he yearns for that beautiful, comforting fiction of religion. But, like his mother, he has long ago decided it was indeed a fiction, maybe the greatest story ever told. When your parents die, that's when you really grow up: there's no longer anyone with unconditional love for you. Except God – if you're religious. He takes on your guilt and sins and forgives you. The way Jack sees it, you can accept this comfort from God, or you can forgive yourself or at least accept yourself (*I'm only human*) or – and this has been his choice – you continue to judge and condemn yourself. He didn't seek amnesia, but he is here to see if an amnesty with himself was possible.

Jack looks up to see a couple walking towards the far end of the beach, their black dog running ahead. The beach is empty of his own people. Blurred seagull shadows on the sand are not the only shadows. There is no rerun, tides ebb and flow. The world turns. In the sun the sea turns, chameleon, from grey to green. Clouds are rushing by. April is the cruellest month. He gets to his feet and walks back across the beach. Stepping onto the track up from the beach, he turns to look back at his two sets of footprints, one out and one back. In a few hours the sea will erase them. Tomorrow others will be there, with maybe the sound of voices and children's laughter. He walks up the track, following in the footsteps of his grandfather and his parents: first parents watched over their children, then children watched over their parents. That, at least, was how it should be. Stopping, he looks back again. He had come here with Branwen, too. Was it four years since they had walked hand in hand, dazzled by their reawakening, leaving their footprints in the sand, then carrying shoes and paddling along the edge of the cold sea? The realisation: he will not be here again. That ache to be loved, despite who he is.

He continues up the track. *The best I can give myself for that part of my life is five out of ten.* His knees are sore, he slows to a plod. A hot bath is all he wants, to soak his tired legs, but in that night's B&B there is no bath, just a shower. Afterwards he goes to the pub for a meal in the bar. He listens in to conversations but speaks to no one. In bed, though weary, he cannot sleep. It is not the memories of his mother that keep him awake, it is Branwen: thinking of her on that beach, of his utter happiness with her. He had never felt so complete since his early years with Kathy. How headlong they had drawn each other in.

★

He and Branwen began to email. At first it was just news: what they were reading, films they'd watched, holidays they'd been on – almost like being at a hairdresser's. But gradually he began to hark back to their time together, asking if she remembered certain meetings they'd had, their days out and, finally, daringly, their times in bed. By this stage Branwen had set up a private email address just for them and their exchanges became more sexually charged.

One day, elated after a long walk in wild wind and rain across the Northumbrian moors, Jack phoned her from the shelter of his car. Before he could control the impulse, he announced:

"I'm in love with you, again."

He waited, suddenly picturing where she might be – at her fitness gym, studying at her Italian lesson, with friends in the bookshop café or even in conversation with her husband. How crass he was! He'd gone too far, caught her off-guard. He sat there, excited by what he'd said but petrified at her likely response.

Eventually she said, "Take care, I don't want you to be hurt."

Was it fanciful of him to sense a smile on her face, an unexpected pleasure? He had no idea what to say.

"I can't talk now," she said. "Bye for now."

But it had been said – for her to deal with as she wished. It was the start. Over the coming weeks their emails became more frequent, more explicit – at least on his part. She never said she loved him but she responded warmly. Soon he christened himself her VIP, her virtual paramour. They developed and relished a relationship that was chaste but not platonic, a courtly love. They made virtual dates: at eleven o'clock, each would be in a café (he found one called Memory Lane) and would think of the other, transferring thoughts through the ether; or each would go out and look at the same moon at the same time, imagining the other.

His life was rich and brimful again: the pent-up excitement of logging on and finding another message, or the deflation of there not being one. He would log on several times a day. Everywhere he went he kept his mobile phone on in case she called him or messaged him – on the train returning from a shopping expedition, from a bus stop. It was a secret life – he told no one, not his friends or his children.

Then they arranged another visit in May. He was going to the Gower and to Dylan Thomas' birthplace in Laugharne but it was all an excuse to see her. He wanted to return with her to one of their favourite walks from thirty years ago and end at Thomas' boathouse. She was as eager as he was and made some rearrangements. She would bring a picnic, she said, and Jack was buoyed by her enthusiasm.

He took the train down and picked her up from her house in Swansea in his hire car. Presumably she had told her husband Hugh of their meeting, but he did not ask. They drove out of the city beyond the motorway and along the winding roads. He felt the tense expectation between them, like the sky before a thunderstorm. Casually she laid her hand on his thigh as she talked. It burned there. He hadn't known what to expect, was full of hope but tentative. It had all been words so far, dreams in cyberspace. He parked at the far end of the almost empty car park by Laugharne Castle and turned the engine off. Silence. He turned to look at her as she turned to look at him. He leaned over to kiss her, softly at first. She responded, her hands gently holding his face and stroking his hair. They pulled apart and looked into each other's eyes, hers sparkling and mischievous. They kissed and looked for a long time, saying nothing.

"Shall we walk?" he asked. "It's called 'Dylan's Birthday Walk' now."

So they got out and, hand in hand, took the path into the woods above the estuary, the day now hot and sunny. There were bluebells, forget-me-nots and red campion. Along the shoulder of Sir John's Hill they reached a ruined house, overgrown with trees, dappled with sunlight. They stepped over the fallen stones and stood in what once had been the living room. There was a fireplace still in the wall on their left and another above it in what would have been a bedroom. Their iron grates were still in place. White cow parsley bloomed up from between the stone. Jack smelled the heat of the sun on the damp earth.

"The legends of green chapels," quoted Jack. "Remember this place? How we kissed and I told you I loved you?"

"Of course I remember."

She turned to him and held him. They kissed with such passion.

"You are pleased to see me," she said, laughing, triumphant.

"I've had that erection since we left Swansea," he said. "I remember you once told me to make love to your mind because it was more responsive than your body."

She laughed. "What bollocks! I remember that kiss. I put my hand down the front of your trousers. I shocked myself but thought, what the hell!"

"How about an action replay?" asked Jack.

"We have to talk about that," she said, holding his hand again and walking on.

Jack saw again the frankness and boldness, her passion and directness that had attracted him in the first place. It was all still there, behind that conservative elegance she had brought to the restaurant at their reunion meeting. But now there was self-control as well as eagerness. The path descended to the fields below the hill. They sat on a bench that had 'It was my thirtieth year to heaven' carved into the back.

"A thirty year gap closed just like that – I feel the same as I did back then," Jack said, his arm around her shoulder.

Turning, Branwen looked directly onto his eyes, and replied:

"I want to fuck you – but I won't."

He remembered an email he had sent her recently, wanting to hear her say exactly that. She had remembered, too. Her openness shocked and excited him. Her eyes laughed as he kissed her and held her hard.

"It isn't the same as thirty years ago, Jack," she said. "I'm happily married now."

"But I don't want to take you away from your marriage, for a start – I'm old, a bad bet, got health problems. Let's not pretend about that. If you left Hugh he would be devastated and you would never get over the guilt. Your children would hate you for it, too, and many of your friends. I only have a few good friends and you would have lost your networks, your social circle and replaced it with nothing. I know all that. I do not want to break your marriage."

She looked at him.

"Don't misunderstand," he continued. "More than anything I want to live with you. I'm sure now that you're my last chance of happiness. I want to lay my head on your lap, rest and be still, feel your fingers stroking my forehead. You

79

would bring me peace. What I would bring you is more of a problem."

"So, what do you want from me?"

"When I'm with you I want to do this, walk, talk, kiss. Open up to you, listen to you. When I'm not with you I want to know I'm in a secret place in your head, treasured there. I need to know you value me."

Above them blackbirds sang unseen in the woods.

"Oh, you're there, Jack," she said, kissing him lightly on the forehead. "But when I email you I sometimes think it's like a woman writing to and falling in love with a man on death row: she has an idealised version of him, the whole situation is impossible, they live in parallel worlds. That kind – this kind – of romantic love is a derangement. It can't be trusted. It's a fever that burns out."

"But it's so rich, Branwen, I'm alive again. I'm like a blind person seeing again. The world is different. All this!" He gestured to encompass the whole landscape. "I feel connected to everything."

He looked out at the brown and black cattle on the salt marsh, the old cocklers' cart track, the bending estuary, hedged fields on the low hills opposite, the blue, hazy ridge of distant mountains.

"That's exactly what I mean: a kind of delirium," said Branwen. "I feel it, too. It's why I'm here. But I think what you do is serial falling-in-love. You did it when you were younger. I'm the proof, aren't I? I'm married for nearly thirty years, never been unfaithful, never even been tempted – until now – even though several men have propositioned me. You've moved from one relationship to another. I think the lives we have led have been the best we could have had – appropriate to our characters. If we had married you would have left me for someone else. I'm sorry, Jack, it's who you are."

"I can't deny it, can I? But I'm older now, I'm different. I've lived alone for five years – except for Megan, of course – for the first time in my life. It must mean something, mustn't it, that after thirty years both of us have these same feelings? Instinctively."

"But, Jack, you don't know me really. We're so different, I'm different from who I was. You remember a twenty-four-year-old body. Now I sag and wrinkle like anyone else my age. I need KY jelly, for God's sake. Reality would break the spell."

"Come on, Branwen," he objected.

"You see," she laughed. "Those are the realities. When I was with you and young I let you define me, now I'm my own person, am stronger. I'm materialistic, too, lazy and vain. I like dinner parties. You'd hate all my socialising."

She pointed with her arms at the scene in front of them.

"You love landscape. I like it, too – but only as a backdrop to being with friends. The friends are more important. With you they'd be a distraction."

"I suppose that's true," he said and, after a pause, "let's find a place to eat."

They carried on until they came to a clearing with a pile of sawn sections of tree trunk, the inner wood bleached pale, the bark still moss-covered. Jack shifted some to make seats for them.

"I thought you should be able to see the rings of growth," said Branwen.

Jack looked closer. "I think the wood has dried out and it's cracking along radial lines.

Leaning back, he stroked her arm, looked up at the nape of her neck, her black hair swaying in the breeze. She turned her face to him.

"Jack, Jack, I love being here with you. You fascinate me, you always did. The things you say and see. And you make me feel younger and lovelier than I really am. I love the idea of being in a romance, treasured and desired by you." She paused. "But I'm wracked with guilt. I'm exploiting my husband's trust in me."

"OK," said Jack, flat and dulled. "You're right. Can we put all that aside for the next couple of hours? Then I'll be gone north again, far away, and you will have some peace."

She put her arm round him. "I loved making the picnic for us, just doing an ordinary thing, a thing that couples do."

She looked at him and saw sadness in his eyes.

"All this talking makes me hungry," she said, taking his hand, kissing him on the cheek. "And you'll be starving."

She unpacked the picnic and gave him a small parcel wrapped in foil. He opened it.

"Buttered bara brith! My favourite. You remembered."

"Of course I did."

After lunch they wandered back along the estuary path, leaning into each other, pausing to kiss, seeing the river twist away beyond the boathouse, the tide ebbing with silver-edged, swirling currents. Two kayaks paddled along the far shore. Somewhere a seal wheezed and coughed. With the sense of an ending, they got back into the car. During the long drive back Jack felt so close to her, so at peace with her. Yet there was an unbridgeable distance between them. The silence in the car grew tense. What next? He had no idea. He had been so happy and now feared the worst.

He stopped outside her house. She had taken her hand from his when they entered the city. He could not read her face as she said goodbye. She waved from her garden gate and he drove off. On the long rail journey home his phone was on the table in front of him but she sent him no texts.

And the weather turned around,
It turned away from the blithe country.

Two days later she sent an email. He had managed to restrain himself from sending any to her, though he had written two and kept them as drafts. Whatever happened, he would prove to her – and himself – that he could be steadfast. He would stay faithful to her. But even as he thought it, he saw how ludicrous this was, pointless. No fool like an old fool. Could he at last love selflessly, in a way that was new to him? It made him feel good about himself. He paused before he opened the email: would the bell toll, or ring out in celebration?

He read:

Dearest Jack,

I loved our time together. Loved it too much. For that reason I must take control of myself again. I will never leave Hugh, I will never sleep with you. I'm sorry, Jack. I know that will hurt you but you have to know. I will cut down on this messaging. It has been taking over my life – I get up in the morning and all I want to know is, will there be a message? When I come back into the house I rush to the computer for the same reason. Hugh has almost caught me, inadvertently, composing a message to you: I was in a state of panic and terror. I dread that I will make a mistake and he will read one of them. He would be so hurt. This is a form of infidelity and it is shaming to him. The good things here have become worthless because my mind is elsewhere. "You seem far away," he said to me today. My guilt burned me up. I must learn to avoid the computer as an addict must avoid drugs, I must ration my message time to you, and make space in my head for what is here, for where my loyalties and real love lie. I want to be honest again, like my husband. I must be less emotionally involved with you. You must understand.

Branwen xx

The inevitable had happened. He did understand. The cruel irony was that he loved her for that decision: it confirmed the qualities he admired in her. The episode with her along the river had been like a visit to the theatre: the action on a brightly lit stage surrounded by the darkened auditorium, a fiction dramatised, the willing suspension of disbelief.

He sent a brief acknowledgement to her message and lapsed into lassitude. But in a couple of weeks she sent another message – chatty, news about her family, enquiries about his. He replied in like tone, safe, non-emotional. But gradually over the next months from both of them there were cautious hints of feelings still alive, hints that drew responses. Warmth returned though Branwen was never as explicit as she had been. It was nearly a year after their day on the Gower when Jack risked saying that he wanted to meet her again. Three messages later she agreed and he made a plan. He was going walking for three days in the Cotswolds and so they could both meet in Stroud and would have most of the day there. Her reason to Hugh was that she was reading Laurie Lee and wanted to see his birthplace in the Cotswolds. Hugh, she knew, wasn't interested and so she would come on a weekday when he was working.

Would it be a painful valedictory? Would the show start again? Jack didn't know: all he wanted was to spend time with her.

Ten days later he was waiting for her on the platform at Stroud station. She stepped down from the train, looked for him and rushed forward, her smile dazzling, and wrapped her arms around him. She kissed him hard, hungrily. All Jack's anxieties vanished in an instant. With other passengers wandering past and talking quietly, he held her close to him, his immediate erection hard against her.

"My paramour, and not so virtual," she laughed.

Jack was astounded, jubilant. All the uncertainties of the last months had disappeared.

"A life of its own, a true indicator," he said.

"Is that an example of what they call muscle memory?" she asked, all mischievously innocent.

"Forever in the fibre of my being. The penis never lies."

"Very indiscriminating, though," said Branwen.

"In this case very discriminating. Instant recognition – he knows his true partner."

This was the bold, reckless Branwen – the flip side to her pragmatic competence. As before, she drew him into her exhilaration. The train pulled away, the station was silent and empty again. She took his hand and they walked towards the café.

"No flapjack, just coffees." She said. "I know I like you cuddly but there's the beginnings of a paunch there."

She patted him on his stomach.

"That's the trouble with you fitness gym fanatics."

"I'm not a fanatic, just want to keep my shape. Vanity not fitness."

"Well, you're succeeding," he said. The same slim legs as of old, the neat breasts.

"I want to hold your hand like real lovers, be carefree. Be a normal couple," she said.

They went to a café in Withey's Yard, hidden away down a black-bricked alleyway. They sat outside in the courtyard under strings of gauze pieces twisted to hang like Tibetan prayer flags. It was as if they were discovering each other again, as if they had stumbled out of a long tunnel into daylight. He dared not ask how she had squared all this with her guilt about Hugh. Was their marriage failing? Were they going through a bad patch? A selfish hope flared in him and then was snuffed out – he did not have the self-confidence to sustain her happiness, to replace what she would have lost. But she said nothing, just chatted, asked him questions. There were silences when they looked at each other's faces, softly stroking fingers.

After coffees they went into a bookshop.

"I need some Laurie Lee postcards and a biography of him. My cover story," she said.

He thought he saw a brief dimming of her good mood but the moment passed. They wandered past the warm gold stone seventeenth-century schoolhouse and the church with its spire and gold clock. Holding hands, they entered the busy farmers' market. They tasted plum doughnuts and pieces of fried Gloucestershire Old Spot sausage. Branwen bought him two bottles of Tom Long and Budding Ale to take back with him.

"It's what I want to do with you," she said. "Just the normal, everyday things, buying food, thinking up meals, choosing birthday presents, buying you a treat."

He felt this lacerating, tantalising hint of how life could be. They stood to watch a middle-aged Japanese man in full evening dress playing the violin on a street corner. It had started to drizzle so his plan for them to walk across one of the commons was thwarted.

"Better find somewhere inside," said Jack.

They found an exhibition of photographs that extended through a series of small rooms in an old house. There were more visitors than they had imagined.

"There aren't many corners, are there?" said Branwen. "I want to take you into a corner and give you a long, lingering kiss."

Jack groaned. "I can't take much more of this. Let's get a hotel room for the afternoon."

"I thought you might come up with that idea. I did, too. The answer's 'no'."

"I would be… honourable. I just want to relax with you. I can't do that here, I need the privacy."

"And I need to stay in a public place. In a bedroom I would lose control of myself. I want you too, you know, but I must not. How can you be so confident? I can't. And if, in the heat of the moment, you lost that sense of honour, you would take me with you over the edge."

But he was certain: if they did make love – commit adultery – her guilt would be so magnified. She would hate herself and then hate him. But then they did find a corner in an empty room. They stood together, she leaning against the wall. They kissed long, with all the old tenderness and desire, melding into each other, arms around each other, all tensions gone. He kissed her eyelids, running his tongue across her lashes, his fingers gentle on her cheeks.

"I have come home," he said. "I feel right with you, Branwen."

She opened her eyes, those soft, dark eyes, and looked at him. Then he saw her glance over his shoulder. He turned. Two teenage girls had come in and were looking at them. Suddenly he saw himself as the girls would see him: an old man, grey hair. A dirty old man. Did he hear one of them mutter "Yuk!" as they left? The spell was broken. Branwen stepped away.

There was a distance between them now, a tension. They left and wandered up the street, pausing at noticeboards with information about meetings. They read about Pilates classes, Circle Dancing, Gentle Shintaido and the Flow of Ki, Intuitive Storytelling, Transformation and Regeneration through Tibetan Buddhist Thangka paintings. There was something artificially companionable about their laughter, a conscious desire to please each other and appear to be on the same wavelength.

"Here's something for you," said Jack, reading a notice in the Natural Health Clinic window. "Embodying Feminine Radiance – for women who want to feel a greater connection to themselves. We will explore how to manifest our deepest longings for love, intimacy, creativity and purpose."

Immediately he knew it was an inappropriate thing to say. Something had changed. He tried to divert her away. "Or there's Anthroposophical Art therapy."

Branwen didn't smile. They found a pub for lunch and ordered sandwiches and beer.

"Wasn't that awful?" she said. "Those kids. They thought we were disgusting, a couple of randy, pathetic OAPs. It made me ashamed of myself."

"Ashamed of being with me?" Pointing out that she was seven years younger than him and not an OAP would have been irrelevant.

"Yes, I suppose I was. Isn't that terrible? I shouldn't be here, Jack. We're both suffering from emotional incontinence. We should be wearing pads. For a time I knew that, when I saw Hugh's torment. It brought me to my senses. But as I reassured him and he relaxed I was tempted again. Wasn't that vile?"

Jack felt helpless. What could he say? He saw the day, the expectations, the brief togetherness, the joy, sliding away.

"This is an impossible situation, Jack. We both know it. It's going nowhere. There's no gain in the way we are. I cannot balance the pleasure with the guilt. You are too important to me but I cannot let you be. That's my torment."

His mind was numbed, Jack gazed unseeing at the few men standing at the bar.

"I'm not what I want to be," she continued. "I do not like being selfish and deceitful."

"But you bring out the best in me," Jack replied. "Some steadfastness at last. Some integrity of feeling. Something I'm not used to – as you know."

She shook her head.

"I fear it's a fiction, Jack, that we have woven between us. A lovely, loving fiction that would shrivel in reality."

"This is real, Branwen. How can you deny the validity of what we feel?"

"What do I feel, Jack? You don't know. You don't know the real me, only your idealisation of me. Perhaps I don't know me either. Is it just that I'm vain and all this attention from you, this adoration, is taking me back to that time when all I wanted was you and to give myself to you – is it just the flattery that has appealed to me?"

"Flattery? Is that all it is?" said Jack, appalled.

"And I led you on. In some of those emails I was teasing you, leading you on because I got a buzz out of your responses. I loved the pleasure and power of turning you on. Even today. Who wouldn't? You wrote some beautiful, beguiling things. I lost all sense of proportion. I was living, like you, in a fantasy world."

He was in the dark, the world shrunk to a silence which only her words pierced.

"I don't believe you. You're telling me it was all ego and vanity? That's not you, Branwen."

"That's what I do mean. It is me, one part of me that you don't want to see. You have been giving me a precious gift, you have been giving me love. I know that and I have treasured it. But I fear it was my vanity it all appealed to."

Jack was in free fall, plummeting down. She was destroying him, flaying him.

"When my kids were growing up I used to tell them not to do anything they had to hide or feel ashamed of. And here I am. It's like I have a demon and an angel on my shoulders, Jack, each whispering into my ear. Each convincing me that what I'm doing is right. Has this been just the cliché of a mid-life crisis? A last breakout, a fling before it's too late, an emotional adventure?"

He couldn't tolerate the words, the benediction of her affection cancelled. She was his only assuager.

"Let's walk," he said. "I can't stand this."

"I'm sorry, Jack. I didn't come here to tell you this. You

89

must know that. But those girls, they suddenly opened my eyes. I know how my husband would see us. Now I know how a stranger sees us. There's nothing right about it."

"You once wrote to me, 'without memory and passion life is meaningless'. Now you're telling me all this is meaningless. I can't believe that."

"No, Jack, it is not meaningless but I must put you away and make room again for Hugh and for my real life."

She was resolved, Jack knew that, and he knew the strength of her will.

"I never wanted to break your marriage. I told you that at the start. I just wanted to be a part of your life, to know that I existed in your mind. Another thing you wrote was that mind to mind was more important than face to face, more important than sex. The intimacy of mind to mind. The stuff I've written to you – you know more about me than any other living person. I've never been able to be like that with anyone – except Kathy in the good years."

"Surely you understand, Jack. Hugh is my husband, a good man. I love him. I will not betray him any longer. And you will be in my mind – in a secret place where I can think of you."

"You know the bleakest thing I've ever read? Beckett, I think. One of his characters says: 'Don't speak to me, don't touch me. Stay with me'."

Branwen made no reply.

"I must get out and walk," said Jack.

The drizzle had stopped and there was a pale grey light. They found the canal towpath and walked along it for the afternoon, mostly in silence though they still held hands, perhaps afraid to acknowledge the finality of what had been said. The canal was derelict, overhung with willows, choked with sedge, mallards paddled about among swirls of green slime and black reflections of tree branches. Bulrushes leaned, the River Froome bubbled past on the other side of the towpath. They stopped at a wooden post which held a piece of slate in which was carved:

"What joy to receive
from each towpath dragonfly
its dismissive glance."

But neither commented, each lost in their own thoughts. They reached a building site where a lock was being renovated. There was an old green caravan and upturned yellow wheelbarrows, metal fencing, squashed cans in the stagnant water. A sign said 'Danger, deep soft mud.' A train roared by, higher up the valley side. At a white and black metal footbridge they turned back and Branwen linked her arm in his. He leaned against her, just wanted to collapse on her. They'd agreed the arrangements. She would leave first and he would catch his train half an hour later. He had not wanted to leave her on the platform, alone and forlorn as he had imagined. The absurdity of life.

They had an hour to wait for her train so they went into a small café for cups of tea. They said little, Jack depressed, unable to think or emerge from an all-encompassing sadness. He saw that Branwen was, if not happy, in a new contentment – as if she was on the mend, confident she had now shaken off the infection, the bug.

"I've just been a side dish, haven't I?" he said bitterly. "An optional extra, which you've paid for with guilt and panic and anxiety. But for me, you were a richness, an added dimension. And don't tell me time is the best painkiller."

"It is, Jack. Remember that I've experienced that – all those years ago when you left me for Laura. She was your fantasy then."

How could he deny it?

"Let's not talk any more," Branwen continued. "It's time for me to go anyway."

Outside the café they stood, Jack paralysed, not knowing how to be. Branwen kissed him on the cheek.

"You're up here," she said, pointing to her head. "Always will be. You're very special."

With that, she walked away to the station. Jack stood looking after her. Would she turn around for a last look, a wave, a change of mind? She did not.

A week later, back home, he received an email from her.

Dear Jack

I felt miserable on that train back from Stroud, guilty about Hugh and about you too. I said some harsh things and some were exaggerated. The flattery and vanity, for instance. It's all impossible. I am sorry, Jack. I hope you can be happy.

Branwen.

Be happy! A sudden flame of jealousy, a helpless rage. Would he be in her head, as she had said outside the café? He needed most of all to be in that secret place in the attic of her mind – something precious to be wrapped carefully in tissue paper, placed on the red velvet in the carved wooden box. Finding a haven there. *You can't fall off the edge of my world,* she had once written. *You're too close to the centre.* To be in her thoughts occasionally, to be thought of softly when she was alone for a moment before she shut out the thought. Was that a kind of love, the only one in fairness that she could offer?

The bind was that he loved her for her return to Hugh, the integrity in that. He was happy that now she could be open and direct, no longer deceitful, being the goodly wife. Was it all no more than a brief encounter, one of millions in the world, now and in the past? Nothing special, just human? Just ordinary?

★

Those two days, two letters. He had soared to the heavens and fallen to the depths. Was it just the passing of time that had helped him survive the four years since then? He told himself it was not: his feelings now were just as intense. He had found a way of managing them, a way which made him feel good about himself. He had created fictions in his head, he knew, sustained some frail hope. Would she be as harsh now as she had been in Stroud, would time have dimmed her memories or softened them? Had she deliberately exaggerated to justify herself, and to make it easier for him to dislike her and therefore forget her?

There had been the occasional email, every three months or so, just holiday news and books to read. She had closed down her special email address, everything was open.

But it turned out not to be quite the final chapter, he said to himself, turning over yet again in his bed to ease the ache in his knees, waiting for light to appear around the curtain, waiting for an ease in his heart. There was another day, another 'final' meeting.

4. WALK, DAY FOUR

Throughout the night, wind batters the B&B bungalow where Jack is staying. He hears the chimes of the grandfather clock in the hall at three and four and five o'clock. At eight o'clock he gets up, opens the curtains and watches the torrential rain hardened by the lashing wind into beads that rattle onto the windows then melt down the glass. He turns on the bedside radio. The whole country is storm-bound, snow on the hills, flash floods in the valleys.

Bugger this! He's long past the stage when weather like this was a challenge he accepted, enjoying the endurance, relishing the discomfort, vain about his persistence. He reviews the day's walk: a long coastline trek that will be completely exposed to the wind beating in from the sea, especially the long curving beach of Penllech. Then the path turns inland, which will give some relief but he knows that countryside is boring – just small fields, hedges with stiles, a couple of caravan sites. He tries to find a motive for going on. There's only one: to be able to say he completed the whole walk. Say to whom? Who's he trying to impress? His children? *Funny how when you're young you want to impress your parents and when you're old you want to impress your children.* Himself? He'd get some satisfaction, yes, be pleased with himself for making the effort, not giving in. He looks out of the window at the swaying, wind-thrashed trees, the greyness, hears the gurgling of gutters and drainpipes, sees rain bouncing off the garden path. *Where's the pleasure in going out in that? Perhaps this is what is meant by the wisdom of old age.* The decision is made: he'll give it a miss.

So he enjoys a more relaxed breakfast, *the fourth of my last six,* requesting more toast and another pat of butter. It is agreed that he can spend the rest of the morning there, repacking his things, reading, waiting for the weather to change and then he will move on to his next hotel around lunchtime. Back in his room he picks up the Platonic solid for the day, the icosahedron: composed of twenty equilateral triangles, five to each vertex. It is the largest of the forms and so Plato associated it with water, denser than fire or air. How appropriate for today. He turns it in his hand, the wood grain of the Japanese cypress like sand ripples across the polished triangles. Symmetry: only the five shapes fulfil the rules of edges, angles and faces. He had hoped this journey would reveal a kind of symmetry, a final harmony. Perhaps he is attracted to symmetry because he has never found it in his life: his life of tangents, wrong turns, broken circles and cul-de-sacs. The geometry of the icosahedron connects it with the faces of the Great Pyramid at Giza and with the golden ratio. From point to line to plane, from circle to globe, from triangle to pyramid, from square to cube; from one to three dimensions – the beauty, clarity and logic. His life, however, is doodles and squiggles, shapeless and formless, approaching – returning to – the final point, and a point – mathematically – is without dimension and not in space, with no inside or outside. Beautifully appropriate. He will have completed a circle around his scrawls. *Is that an accomplishment? At least the completion will be done at a time of my choosing. It will be intentional.*

He reads and snoozes the rest of the morning. For some reason, maybe connected with the snow, he recalls being with Kathy in snow-covered Wenceslas Square in Prague, drinking mulled wine and then wandering over the Charles Bridge and listening to the jazz band there. How much he had wanted to travel to other places with her, carried along by her enthusiasm, to share quiet places.

Around one o'clock, the rain and wind ease. He arranges for a taxi to pick up his luggage and then him later that afternoon at the church of Llangwnnadl, and sets out to walk there. Looking to the north he sees snow on Yr Eifl and further north still the Snowdon range is white. Branches torn from the trees lie across the lane. He picks up a pine cone – his token for the day – conker shiny, rough, knobbly scales closed against the rain.

The church – the next heading south on the pilgrims' trail from Tudweiliog – sits picturesque in a sheltered glade by a river, not far from the sea. Inside it is clean and well looked after, light, well attended too. Spacious with a double knave, there's a lovely Easter garden just inside the door, hassocks bright and individually embroidered, a table of cards and flowers. It's a living place, Jack feels, an odd mix of energy and peace.

Outside in the churchyard there is a wooden bench by the river – swollen, brown and rushing. Jack wipes the seat dry and unwraps his ham and tomato sandwich, drinks some hot coffee. Time for his next contemplation, one that compels him back to his first fundamental failure.

*

Jack and Tom waited obediently with the other visitors in the small over-heated hallway of the maternity hospital. A nurse came, wedged the doors open and they all hustled into the corridor.

"This one, Dad," said Tom.

They turned into the small side ward. Tom's wife, Bethany, was sitting up in bed, her baby, Peter, to her breast, cradled in her arm. Bethany looked up and Jack saw big black bruises under her eyes, her usual tanned face pale, her hair awry. He could see only the baby's dark hair. Tom bent and kissed her forehead. She looked at Jack and smiled, but it was a weary smile.

Watching her, Jack had another picture in his mind: the photograph he had taken of Kathy similarly sitting up in a hospital bed holding baby Megan whom he had just placed in her arms. He could never forget Kathy's smile of achievement and happiness as she too looked down at her new child.

He now watched Tom stroking his baby son's dark head. Any man's child is his second chance. His son understood that. But Jack hadn't. Forty years ago Jack had committed the first great betrayal of his life. Back then there was no place for a man at birth. His son, Tom, had been delivered by a midwife who had galloped through a snowstorm to the nursing home where his first wife, Vicky, was in labour. Jack had waited at home for the phone call.

"Mr. Richards?"

"Yes?"

"You have a baby son."

His heart beating hard, his first question was: "Is he all right?"

In the answer seemed to lie all his future.

"He's fine, and his mum too."

He was not allowed to speak to his wife, there were only the set visiting hours. He put the phone down and collapsed, weeping with relief. His son was healthy, Vicky was fit and well, Abi had a brother, he had a family. But there was the horror of what he had to do. For now there was another woman, Helen, a work colleague he had become close to during the last few months. They had met secretly in pubs, kissed in the car in dark city backstreets; but they had not made love. With some last twisted sense of morality he had drawn the line there. Somehow he had to tell his wife she and their new son and their daughter had to go, back to her parents.

The next evening, after a day of appearing to work, he went to visit them. He grasped his wife's hand and tears were in his eyes, tears for her but tears also because of his new loathing of

97

himself, for his imminent betrayal of her. She looked so happy and proud. But where was this son, this Tom? With the other new fathers he had to go downstairs and stand in a line in the corridor. On the other side of a large internal window a nurse held up each child in turn and called its name. Sheepishly, with unnatural restraint, each father stepped up, looked at his new child and made some gentle inarticulate sound. The nurse turned briskly away for the next baby. Jack looked at the tiny swaddled figure. It was incomprehensible, what he knew he was going to do. It was a cruelty he had not known he was capable of. He looked at Tom and knew he loved him. Yet he looked too with a callous dispassion. For there was something more powerful in his life, something that drove him, enabled him to do this. Something he lacked with his wife, Vicky, but had discovered with Helen.

That something enabled him to pack up the car three days after Vicky and baby Tom came out of the nursing home, pack the baby clothes and the baby gear and Abi's favourite toys, pack his wife's clothes and drive for two hours with his wife sitting beside him and his son in the back in a carry cot, his beloved daughter in the car seat.

No wonder, Jack thought as he watched the grown-up Tom so tender with his wife and child, that self-hatred had dominated his life since then. How could he have left his new, days-old son and toddler daughter and abandoned his wife who had shared so much with him? He had left them at her parents, forbidden by them to cross the threshold. How could he have returned on his own to a barren house so recently full of life and hope?

He had visited them every weekend. In Greenbank Park he had walked Tom in his pram, holding hands with Abi. They sat in cold shelters, fed the ducks on the pond. He chatted to his children, saw their eager curiosity and then returned them to the in-laws' house, handed them over to Vicky on the doorstep. How could he have done that? How could he have said goodbye and driven off? How could he have failed to imagine the scene when he left? He wanted so much to expiate his callousness by renewing his family. And yet... and yet... even then, even as he looked with often-tearful eyes at his small son and lovely daughter, he sensed a deep restlessness that had been awakened in him and that was still with him – almost a kind of recklessness.

He had some unshakeable feeling – not thought or anything logical – that some key part of him could not flourish in that family set-up. The appearance of Helen on the scene had brought alive an independent individual, newly conscious of how so far his life had been moulded for him. He remembered the pivotal scene when, from a bedroom window, he had watched Vicky, already bulging with a baby, playing with Abi in the garden. Vicky looked complete, fulfilled in herself. He hadn't felt the same – not because of Abi and the new baby or even Vicky – but because he felt his life so far had been laid down for him: school, university, engagement, job, marriage, child. This was the progress blessed by society – a conveyor belt of expected stages. Looking back, he seemed now to have had no say in it, been unable to step outside it and make his own choices. He didn't blame anyone: it was just normal, what happened. But he hadn't had the individuality to question it or break the rhythm. Helen, a choice of his own, was giving him a new perspective. It was an answer he now found even more untenable – his selfishness might explain but could not justify. It had caused a self-loathing which had never left him.

The adult Tom knew what was important: the ties that held him with his wife and with his new son, Peter. Later Tom would tell Jack about watching his son's first sleep at home: his miniature perfection, soft skin, petrol eyes, his faint whimpers, his little finger gripped by the baby's tiny hand. At two months Peter slept on his tummy, slept in Tom's arms, in a sling on walks in the snow. His first smile – not the first communication but the first mutual one – the baby's sense of him. The first lifting of the head to look around, lying on his blanket watching his hands moving in front of his face, fingers flexing, screaming purple-faced in the bath, asleep in his cot, fist curled on his pillow next to his ear.

Later still Jack would watch Peter's commando crawling, propelling himself forward on hands and knees, awkward as an iguana, eager, curious, enthusiastic, joyful screeches and cries, pigeon-like coos, smiles and chortles. He hid his face behind chairs, then laughed at the "boo!" He put the cushion over his face to hide. He showed off with delight at his cleverness and skills: bashing the table with a plastic spoon, opening a cupboard though he already knew he shouldn't, exploring shoes and laces, slippers, picking them up and turning them over, putting his hand and arm inside, demanding attention, with great patience and concentration pouring and measuring lentils with different-sized spoons into different-sized containers. In the baby bouncer Peter was astonished and thrilled at his own jumping and turning, yelping and laughing. Jack had renounced all that experience with baby Tom.

One afternoon Peter had tipped over a standard lamp, which had then fallen on him. He had been told "no!" But now Jack watched him crawl to it again. Peter stretched out his hand towards its grey metal base.

"No!" said Jack.

He looked at Jack, his hand halted in mid-air.

"No!" Jack repeated.

Peter's fingers hovered over the lamp base, flexing, getting lower but still not touching. He looked up at Jack again.

"No!" Jack repeated for the third time.

Peter took his hand away, moved to the side.

"Good boy!" said Jack.

Peter's hand now played with the radiator thermostat

wheel. As he played he turned to look at Jack. He knew precisely what he was doing. He knew this was OK and he had saved his face. *How young kids are independent, want to challenge and defy.*

And Helen? Like Branwen much later, she had returned to her husband, fearful he would not survive without her, drawn back by his need. He had damaged his children for nothing, opened up a split from Vicky that would never heal.

★

He was filled with disgust for himself, unable to scrub the stain clean. This, above all, was why he was making this final journey.

How have I learned to live with myself? Shallowness is my saving grace.

Jack takes a drink of coffee. It is tepid, sour. He throws it into the stream. He stands up and watches the water go gurgling by. *Unconscious, just travelling on, impelled only by gravity, purposeless. The simplicity of it. The unintended peace, the accidental beauty.*

He had managed to create another life with Kathy and have another child, Megan. *How can I do that? How am I able to shift the past aside and carry on, start again?* This ability to live with himself is a second cause of self-contempt. He must lack some basic component of being human – something like compassion, something like the ability to truly love. No matter how he looks at it, he finds no other way to understand it. A callous selfishness is his core emotion.

He had denied Tom twice: just after his birth, and then again when he left the family home. As Vicky had said, he had not made the effort. But Tom had been a baby at the first denial, only two years old at the second. Abi had been older, old enough to sense what was happening, to comprehend her rejection by her own father. That was far worse. And yet she too had forgiven him. How much he had taken from them when he had turned his back on them, disowned them, discarded them. Yes, he had tried hard afterwards, had kept faith with them with regular visits and holidays. They could depend on him for those things. He always kept promises, never let them down; he made and kept arrangements.

Jack looks back at the little church. Would there be a third betrayal? And would the cock crow?

And the greatest miracle? That Abi is a truly loving person with integrity at her core; that his son, Tom, so unlike him, so obviously capable of truly loving, is tender. He thinks of Megan at university. Was she poring over her laptop, researching in the library, laughing with her friends, playing squash? She was certainly developing a ready wit and repartee.

He looks at the simple pastoral scene around him. How could he be entranced by the movements of a bird or be moved by a landscape, weep at suffering or heroism on TV – and yet have abandoned his children and their mother, Vicky, at her most vulnerable and needy time? *I am not worthy.*

Anyone who knew his story would despise him. Only he knew it fully and so he despised himself. This ridiculous self-assessment he was undertaking would only come to the conclusion he already knew. The story of Branwen was the other side of his coin, the biter bit, the balancing out, the turn of the wheel. It seemed he could keep faith only with an impossible, unreal love – a fiction he had created for himself, as others here in this place had created their own fiction out of Christ. Inside the church was the Easter garden, the greenery of resurrection and rebirth. *A wonderful dream, but not for me. I'm too far gone for rebirth.*

He had been granted one rebirth already, at the cruellest cost. Kathy had given him that chance of some redemption:

her death had given him the full responsibility for Megan. Had he truly required such a shock to jolt him into what was natural for most people – loving? He remembered how Kathy had played with the young Abi and Tom as if they were her own children, tumbling off sledges with them, dramatising her storytelling with gestures and a range of accents. She had so much love to give; loving was natural to her.

He remembered how, in the shade of the spinney, he and Kathy had watched Abi. Jack felt such a love for her: simple, uncomplex, accepting. The sun was hot and blazed down as she rode her pony bareback across the hard dry green field. There was a makeshift jump of battered oil drums and broken pieces of coloured board. Her aim was to get her pony, Zephy, to jump it. She cantered him round the edge of the field to warm him up. Three times he approached the jump but, at the last second, sidestepped it and then – just to prove his point – bolted to the far corner of the field.

Abi walked him back to us. Kathy gently stroked Zephy's head, talking to him softly. Her love of animals was something Jack loved, she seemed to have an affinity with natural things.

"You bloody pest!" muttered Abi. Jack knew the strength of her will. "He won't do anything this afternoon. He's getting a real sweat up. Zephy! Come on."

She yanked the reins and dug in with her boots. He moved off reluctantly, at his own pace. But she would master him. At the fourth attempt, he did it. In triumph she cantered off with him, blonde hair streaming out, moving easily with the flow of the horse.

"She's a determined young woman, your daughter," said Kathy.

Later they moved into the shade and cool of the stable with its smell of dung and leather. Abi groomed Zephy: long, sweeping strokes down his flanks, carefully on his head, combing out the mane. She was totally absorbed in him, fulfilled, thought Jack. She fussed over him with pony nuts and salt licks, fly fringes and over-boots. But it was also a genuine looking after because she alone was responsible for him, at twelve years old. She gets rid of his ringworm, shoes him, rises at 6am in the dark, cold winter to go down and see him before school, to turn his hay and feed him. At the end of the day, after another ride in the cool evening, she will give him a last rub-down and a bucket of pony nuts. She has proudly told Jack of Zephy's Arab blood which shows in the high way he holds his tail when he canters.

Vicky and Justin only allowed Jack to visit once every three weeks. He loved his time with them, but it was an excruciating pleasure: the immense difficulty of switching feelings off after he'd seen them.

Jack had another memory.

At Spring Bank Holiday he and Kathy took Abi and Tom to a cottage near Jervaulx Abbey in the Yorkshire Dales. One day Kathy had taken Abi off to Richmond to do some food shopping. Jack had taken Tom down to the river and Tom had wanted to go off on his own. After two hours he came strolling back under the alders along the curving bank of the River Ure, his black metal-detector foraging in front of him, dials glinting in the bright sunlight.

"I didn't find anything Roman, Dad, but I've got two old cartridges. I deliberately did a sudden run out of the field, pretending I'd found something valuable."

Jack laughed. Tom's wit and enthusiasm were unquenchable. Earlier that morning they'd looked at a large-scale map and seen, in the fields by Fleet House: 'Human remains, knife and ornaments found AD 1884'. So Jack had dropped him off by the church at the start of the public footpath.

"It's like an adventure, Dad, going off on my own," he'd said.

Jack had been nervous about letting him go but also

wanted to encourage his independence. Tom was to traverse some fields and ask at the House for permission to look. They had given him permission but told him the site was now a dump; if he were to find anything valuable he was to take it back to them. Now he was safely back.

"Come in for a swim, Dad, please."

"It's too cold for me," but Jack felt churlish, guilty about disappointing him. Instead they built a stone pyramid in the river and threw stones at it from the bank, carefully calibrating their aim but always missing it.

"Challenge you to a stone-throwing competition, Dad. Who can throw furthest?"

They hurled pebbles down the river and Jack decided he must win so as not to be patronising, and Tom would know anyway if he was cheating to lose. But he would win by only a small margin.

"You've got a good throwing arm, Tom."

"I'm going up to the cottage to get my fishing net. Shall I bring the cricket bat as well?"

"Yes, good idea."

So many things Tom wanted to share with him – activities, enthusiasms. He had a questing, curious brain.

Tom came back and began to rake among the pebbles on the riverbed.

"Hey, Dad, I've found another buckle."

He lobbed it up to Jack.

"Look at it, it's not leather that goes through it. Must be something special."

Under every oak and yew tree Tom saw a potential hoard of a merchant's buried wealth. No failure blunted his imagination. Jack knew he could wilt under Tom's expectations. He knew he failed him when he didn't participate but there was a difficult balance between joining in and letting him be. Jack was sure he got it wrong. These brief times together were so concentrated: there was a kind of desperation – from both sides, he felt – to get things right so as not to displease or disappoint. What was missing was the comparative relaxation of daily living together, the natural rhythms of people fitting round each other, periods of closeness and separateness naturally evolving. Always, also, was the fear of being diminished from 'father' to 'kindly uncle who organised treats'.

Jack followed Tom to see him fishing upstream. But instead he saw his greenish shape swimming under the surface of a deep pool. Shadowed under the thick alders, the water was the colour of old leather.

"Come on in, Dad."

Jack stooped to feel the water with his hand.

"Ah, Tom, it's too cold. Why do you want me to come in?"

"It's more fun with you. I like to see you getting cold. I like the look on your face when you go under for the first time."

"Good enough for me, Tom."

So Jack stripped off his T-shirt and shorts and waded in in his underpants.

"Do you think there are any pike in here, Dad?"

They swam in the deep pool then turned into canoes, tumbling in single file on their stomachs down the white-water rapids to the next pool. A couple of hikers, with neat green rucksacks on their backs, watched them from the bank. *Doing walks for motorists,* thought Jack.

Jack waded out and Tom went back to enlarge the pyramid of stones. Jack took his camera to find the right angle to photograph him. He wanted to capture Tom's happiness in himself, alone in a large landscape, piling his stones as the river curved away through the fields with Middleham Low Moor in the distance. Like any child, Tom lived in the moment, able – Jack was sure – to activate the other major part of his life when he stepped over the doorstep of his home at the end of a trip like this. Unconsciously – Jack hoped – it was a strategy both Tom and Abi would have had to learn. Jack himself had not learned it: these vivid interludes were brilliant with fragile emotion. Often, on the drive home, Jack's nerve would fail: it all seemed pointless, fragments with no pattern.

"I'll offer you a skimming contest," shouted Jack.

But Tom maybe didn't hear him and continued happily skimming alone. Then he came up the bank with a heavy stone in his hand.

"Dad, Geoff Capes!"

He shot-putted the stone back into the river.

"Do you think there's enough wind to fly a kite?"

Jack looked at the moving tops of the trees.

"Yes, I think so."

"Will you help me launch it? It's a stunt one and it's got a thirty-foot red tail. Justin bought it for me."

Justin – that stab.

"OK. Will you go up to the cottage and get it then?"

"Right, will you time me?"

Always testing himself. He refastened the always-undone laces of his trainers and then raced off.

"Three and a half minutes," announced Jack when Tom returned. "Pretty good."

The stunt kite had two strings, which were inevitably tangled up.

"You're good at untangling, Dad."

It was one of those skills fathers were supposed to have. Half an hour later they got the kite into the air. Jack spent the rest of the afternoon along the riverbank in his damp underpants flying the kite with Tom. He had never learned to do it as a child, self-conscious in front of spectators as the kite crash-landed, his own father berating his stupidity.

Eventually they pulled in the kite, tied the strings neatly and sat by the river, eating chocolate that Jack had saved.

"I like it by rivers, Dad. I like listening to the water."

So they listened to the water and watched two cows come down to drink. Two grouse landed in the cornfield behind them and disappeared. They packed up all the kit Tom had accumulated, including the old belt buckle and the cartridges, and walked up to the cottage.

"I wonder if the girls will be back," said Jack.

"But it's my turn to do the bacon butties for tea."

"Sure is, Tom."

Along the path Tom suddenly stops and says: "Wouldn't it be funny, Dad, if we were really living in a dream and when we die, we wake up?"

Jack thought a bit. "Depends," he said.

After all that, one out of ten was all he could award himself. The one because surely Vicky had had a part to play in the failure of their marriage.

The wind had dropped now and grey mist was low over the hills. It was too early to call the taxi so Jack looked at the map and found a circular walk along the country lanes. Walking in the damp air, raindrops on leaves, water gurgling in ditches, he recalled his last proper meeting with Branwen.

★

Living on his own, things were simpler: Jack could keep faith with Branwen. When the emails began again, Jack sensed something below the surface gossip (for that is what their emails largely were, each on guard against any greater import). Branwen was being loyal to her husband but was unable to fully resist what drew her to Jack. Jack saw she needed to communicate with him and her conflict was a kind of balm to him, selfish though he knew that was. Maybe it was just nostalgia. In his messages he risked the occasional sentence about missing her, that he could not imagine never seeing her again. She ignored those statements. Then he told her about

108

his fibrillating heart and the electric shock procedure that was planned in a couple of months' time. Even as he wrote the simple fact, he knew it was a kind of emotional blackmail. Was he sinking to new depths? He told her he was coming down to Manchester to the Lowry Centre. Was there any chance of meeting there? Lowry was one of his favourite artists.

Her reply was a long time coming. She had been very busy, she said, but, yes, she would come and suggested a particular date. She had created a suitable cover story for Hugh. Jack was elated but there was something clinical in the tone of the email that made him apprehensive: was this to be some kind of formal farewell or was it a sympathetic gesture towards his heart condition? Excited but wary he booked his train tickets.

Jack was early, of course. In his state of heightened excitement, he was amazed and thrilled by the architecture of Salford Quays: the new media centre, the shining steel curves of the Imperial War Museum, the adapted warehouses, the variety of architectural styles. There was a vibrancy and energy and self-confidence – in sharp contrast to his inner apprehension. Now as he loitered on the cobbles outside the theatre/gallery all his pessimism returned: so much anticipation was bound to end in disappointment; such a brief time they would have, five hours.

He stood there not knowing the reaction he would get. Then he saw her crossing the white curving bridge over the canal. She saw him and waved. He hurried towards her, saw her smile and then embraced her, feeling her arms around his neck and kissed her, felt her kiss him back, the softness of her lips, felt himself relax into her, let the tension go. But the kiss was briefer than he wanted. She pulled away to look at him.

"I'm not late, am I?"

"Not at all, but I could do with a coffee."

She linked her arm in his as they walked back to the theatre. He was happy, wanted it always to be like this, the two of them

109

making a visit, a couple glad to be together, interested in each other's opinions, no subterfuge. In spite of his apprehension, a sense of their rightness together filled him. They entered the building.

"Wow, the colours – and the floors slope. It's making me feel seasick," she said.

He loved it: the low-ceilinged, curving catacomb with orange and sunflower-yellow walls, the long stretches of purple and orange. Bold, simple, no gradations. In the Tower Café Jack bought coffees and a piece of apple cake.

"To share," he said. "It's three pounds a slice."

"Big spender," said Branwen.

"I'll cut, you choose," he said.

"And ever the democrat."

She chose the slightly larger piece. They both laughed. But then there was a silence. They had come so far, felt and written and maybe hidden so much over the months and now, though their fingers touched between the plates, he sensed discord between them.

"It's so much easier for you," she began. "You're on your own. No one to lie to, no conflicts."

He knew it. He waited for the axe to fall.

"Yesterday morning at breakfast, Hugh suddenly said he would like to come with me. While I was in the Lowry he could join a guided tour round Old Trafford and then we could have lunch together."

Lamely, Jack said he didn't know Hugh was a United fan.

"He's not but it's a famous football place and he's never been. He does follow football."

"What did you say?"

"I was panicking, heart thumping like mad. I couldn't let him see my face in case he read something into it. I just started to load the dishwasher. Then he added, 'but unfortunately I can't: got this meeting with the big cheeses that I can't get out of'. I closed my eyes in relief. 'Anyway,' he continued, 'I think you just want a day on your own, a bit of space, and that's fine'. I felt awful, Jack. He's such a trusting man. He's so open himself and I used to be the same."

Jack had no answers. He squeezed her hand but there was no response. He heard other couples chatting quietly, the hum of the perpetually padding escalator, noticed how the colours of the cups and saucers echoed those of the walls and décor. Felt defeat. He had wanted to say so much, tell her face to face what he had so far only been able to write. Wanted to explain how they could continue, how he had found a way that he hoped would work for both of them. Could he lever himself up out of this misery, restore the day?

"But still I'm here," she said, taking his hand. "I wanted to see you in spite of all that. And I'm glad to be with you, old misery guts. Let's go see the pictures."

She stood up and kissed him briefly on the lips. Jack marvelled at how she could decide how to be and then just be it.

"Now, wasn't this Lowry a miserable bugger as well? Is that why you like him?"

She just swung him along, ignored his moods, coping with him as presumably she did with Hugh – that capacity could save them, it was the basis of the modus vivendi he had worked out so they could continue. They wandered into the gallery, past walls covered with blown-up black-and-white photographs of the 40s and 50s: football crowds of men in flat caps and trilbies, kids in round NHS glasses, fathers in suits with rolled-up trousers paddling in the sea at Morecambe, poor kids in ragged jerseys playing in narrow backstreets. Jack looked at the hugely magnified faces, saw poverty but also a wistful hopefulness – maybe at the end of the war.

"I was alive then, probably just started school," he said, nodding at the photos.

"Already part of history," Branwen laughed. She was seven years younger than him.

"I like that one," she said, standing in front of 'Man Lying on a Wall'. "The brolly propped up next to the briefcase by the wall, him just lying there along the top, having a fag, hat on his belly, staring up at the clouds. Not thinking. Or perhaps he is. That erect mill chimney behind him seems suspiciously placed."

"Maybe he's thinking of you," ventured Jack. But Branwen ignored the remark.

"Now that's a miserable bunch of folk," she said, pointing at another painting.

"It's supposed to be. It's called 'A Funeral Party'. That's why they're all in black."

Branwen looked more closely. "It's a group but look how separate they all are: nine of them all looking forward, not at each other and he's painted it so that none of their bodies overlap. Nobody's touching anyone."

"*Everyone is a stranger to everyone else.* That's what he thought," Jack said.

"That's nonsense. Don't start. Are you and your kids strangers? Were you and Kathy strangers?"

Jack was still looking at the painting. He said: "The answer to both your questions is 'yes'. My kids are adults and have gone their various ways. They are their own people. I don't know what goes on in their heads, even less in their emotions, any more than they know what goes on in mine, thank goodness."

"I suppose you may be right. Hugh certainly doesn't know what goes on in mine. Perhaps Lowry's right."

"But it's OK, though, isn't it?" said Jack. "I think we need secrets, thoughts and feelings we don't tell anyone. That way we keep our individuality, we stay sane, not compelled to share and explain and justify everything, make other people scared or worried."

He knew he was on thin ice here, like the sour-milk-coloured frozen lake in front of the smoky industrial landscape in the next painting. But Branwen didn't respond.

"This is my favourite," said Jack. They were in front of 'The Derelict House'.

"God, it's so miserable!" said Branwen. "But then that's why you like it."

"Yes, I suppose it is. The one house, narrow like a wedge. What genius to place it on a curve in the road. It just emphasises all the other straight lines, the sharpness. The mill chimney you can see through that hole in the broken fence. And the grey broken house has that red door – lost hope, maybe? And the man standing there, on his own, stooping, maybe remembering or probably doing his best to forget. Everything a dirty white."

"You are bloody morbid, Jack. Maybe we are all strangers but it doesn't mean to say we're all lonely and miserable like that bloke. I'm not, for one. Most of the people I know aren't."

"So far as you know," said Jack. "'All my people are lonely', Lowry said, 'I cannot make people look cheerful.'"

"That's because he was lonely, a miserable old git. No kids, no family, lived with his mother who made him feel guilty and a failure, living in that dark house with all the ticking clocks telling different times. When he died they went into his bedroom and his bed was surrounded by all those paintings by Rossetti – romantic women in thin flowery dresses looking languid. He was seriously weird, I'd say."

"You have done your research, haven't you?" laughed Jack, stimulated by her anger, putting his arm around her shoulder. It was her optimism and straightforwardness he loved.

"I had to, didn't I? To convince Hugh I was coming for the art," her voice suddenly hard. Jack, taken aback, dropped his arm.

They moved on silently into the last room and stopped in

front of 'Two People', a small oil painting on plywood: a man and a woman, dressed all in black apart from the man's dull-blue muffler, both stooping and small, looking at something outside the picture, expressionless, isolated on that familiar dirty-white background, almost floating because there was no demarcation between ground and background.

"Again, not touching," said Branwen. "Always that bloody space between them. I've had enough. That just bloody sums it up."

"'Every man is an island': that was another of Lowry's beliefs," said Jack. "One of mine, too, always has been since I read the opposite in one of John Donne's poems, 'No man is an island'."

He felt it now, a tension between them, a space widening.

"Yes, I know, like that other favourite reversal of yours: 'Man made God in his own image'. I don't know whether it's clever or flippant. And I need a pee."

Turning to go, she said, "This was the right place to meet, after all."

The statement desolated him.

"See you in the gift shop," he managed to say as she strode away.

He needed some token, some symbol of their being together for this brief time, something to recall their stolen meeting, something for both of them. He bought two identical mugs, glazed with Lowry's painting, 'Britain at Play'. He had them quickly wrapped and put in a carrier bag before Branwen returned. He stuffed the bag into his holdall.

"I fancy some lunch," Branwen announced on her return, a briskness back in her voice but she did not take his hand. They passed by Café Rouge, which he thought looked pleasant enough, and entered the Lowry Outlet Mall. He was looking for a place with some privacy in booths, low lights, a bit of atmosphere. But they ended up in the Food

Court in a café opposite Burger King and Harry Ramsden Express. Big screens above the mall were showing golf and tennis. Branwen had chosen this place, turning into it decisively. It was open, with wood-grain laminate tables and upright chairs in straight lines, functional. Two other middle-aged couples, in matching jackets and with M&S shopping bags, were seated. Jack found it utterly depressing. They ate sandwiches; he had a decaf cappuccino, she a latte. They reverted to the neutral ground of recent holidays and what their children were doing. It was matter-of-fact. No mention was made of Lowry. Jack was waiting for the sentence to be passed. He was silent and Branwen was talking too much.

"When Hugh retires in six months," she suddenly said, "he'll be at home all day and I won't be able to get on the computer. I'll have no private time and I won't be able to get away like this."

Had she come to the inevitable decision during the morning, or on the train here, or sitting at home?

"The last time, as I travelled home on the train," she continued, "I was terrified all the way. That Hugh had accidentally found one of my emails to you that I hadn't properly deleted, that he'd got an IT whizz kid friend in and they'd hacked in and found everything. By the time I drove up to the house I was expecting my suitcases to be in the porch. Where this is concerned, I know Hugh would have no grey areas. This is the flip side of his trust."

"But... " began Jack.

"I know, we haven't slept together. But we nearly did, and I have in my mind, many times. And that's just as bad."

Jack visualised them at their corner table, a dislocated couple, staring past each other, silent now.

"Let's go outside," he said. In petty defiance he bought two flapjacks on the way out.

The sun was shining and there was a slight breeze. They chose a bench overlooking the dock basin where a pleasure trip boat was moored, available for party hire. He gave her her flapjack. They munched them, watched joggers pass, young executives cross the bridge from Media City, lanyards with identity passes round their necks. Lone men sat on steps eating sandwiches.

"Look up there," said Jack, desperate for something to talk about, putting off the moment.

On a balcony of the fourteenth floor – he counted them – of a tower block of flats was a pink Wendy house.

"Sad, isn't it?" he said, "to be so confined."

"Making the best of it," she countered.

"I brought this," said Jack. "I wanted us to listen to it together."

Even as he said it, he knew it was hopeless, a romantic idea now shattered. He took out his MP3, gave her an earphone. They sat together on the bench, warmed by the sun, chilled by the breeze, the MP3 between them, looped together by the earphones. He switched it on.

"It's Bob Dylan," he said.

He had imagined them listening to this together in a dark, warm corner of a pub, she resting her head on his shoulder, holding hands, dreaming.

Well I've been to the mountain and I've been in the wind
I've been in and out of happiness
I have dined with kings, been offered wings
And I've never been too impressed.

All right, I'll take a chance, I will fall in love with you
If I'm a fool you can have the night, you can have the morning too
Can you cook and sew, make flowers grow
Do you understand my pain?

Are you willing to risk it all
Or is your love in vain?

I've been burned before and I know the score
So you won't hear me complain
Will I be able to count on you
Or is your love in vain?

The final notes of the guitar faded. He turned it off. She did not move, they sat there, still linked by the earphones. How ludicrous it sounded now. How stupid he had been, in his dreams. He looked across at the reflections of buildings in the deep-blue glass-walled office block opposite. She took the earphone out and handed it back to him.

"I'm sorry, Jack. It has amazed me – you have taken me back to when I was younger. My feelings for you came back, after all these years. But I love Hugh, he is my husband. He's a good, honourable, trusting man and I am being cruel to him, deceiving him. I know I've told you this before. I am shaming him. I hate myself for it. I've always been an open person, honest. You know that. And I want to be that again."

"I understand," said Jack. "That's the bind, what I can't find a solution to: that these qualities, your love and loyalty and needing to be honest, are what I love about you. And what divide you from me. I hoped we could have something else, something that enriched both of us."

"A bit on the side, as they say."

"No, not that," he said bitterly. "Nothing as tawdry as that, nothing like that. Something fine, not tarnished. Jesus!"

"Not possible, Jack. Someone always gets hurt. Like you hurt me those years ago. No, don't say anything. I got over it a long time ago and I've forgiven you. That's all you wanted wasn't it, at first – forgiveness?"

Jack nodded. Things were coming full circle, there was a symmetry.

"Remember when you phoned me after you'd come down the mountain? You said, 'I've fallen in love with you again'. You sounded so full of excitement, so happy. But remember what I said: 'Be careful you don't get hurt'."

"Yes, I do remember and I remember how it felt, as if I'd been given a second chance. But hurt is what it's all about. Hurt is what you get when you want to live too much. Hurt's OK, it's a given."

She turned to look at him. He saw her black eyes, soft again.

"Jack," she said, stroking his fingers. "I could say things, but I won't. I've written enough of them to you in the past. But this must stop. I will never forget these times. But I must put them away. I have said that before as well, but this time I mean it."

She stood up.

"I'm going to get an early train. It's for the best."

Jack stood up too, resigned.

"I bought something for you. I wanted us to remember today, before it turned out as it has."

He gave her the mug and she unwrapped it.

"I bought one for me, too," he said, "the same."

"Thank you."

She rewrapped it in the tissue paper and put it into her bag.

"And now it must be goodbye."

She kissed him on the lips and immediately walked away. He watched her walk fast across the cobblestones towards the bridge, started to follow her, watched her as she reached the bridge. He stopped as she went up the slight incline, watched as she went down the other side towards the glittering copper-roofed building. He waited to see if she would turn, pause and wave. She did not. She turned a corner out of sight.

She would leave the mug somewhere: in the station, on the train, not wanting a daily reminder because she would want to forget. He wanted only to remember. He stared down into the grey canal.

On his own return train journey he desperately wanted to text her, to try and retrieve what had turned out to be a disastrous day. He saw them both sitting on trains travelling in opposite directions, further and further away from each other, staring glumly out of the window – or would she be feeling relieved? If he texted and she did not reply he would feel worse.

Three long days later he received an email:

Jack,

On the train home I asked myself with disbelief, what had I been doing up there in Manchester? I wanted only to get back to safety, to my husband, my family and friends and my real life where I belong. To being again the straightforward person I used to be. I was so wrong to agree to a meeting – but maybe right because it brought things to a head. I have been confused for a long time but now I have shaken my head and it has cleared. Here at home I am in the familiar complacencies, if you like, in the ordinary. I love Hugh totally. Perhaps this time with you has proved that to me, however interesting I think you are. Hugh is interesting, too, and principled. He is an honest, trusting man and I never want to lose his love and respect. I feel for him the kind of love that I think you feel only for your children. I have betrayed him and now must show him I love him even more. I must heal my marriage. I cannot lose him. For that reason, we must never meet again. This is final. Please do not reply. I am sorry, Jack.

Branwen. xx

Jack read and reread the message, hoping to find a code within its brevity that gave him some hope. The two kisses – were they a parting gift, a farewell? It was inconceivable that he had seen her for the last time and that the last time had been so cruel, so unsatisfactory.

Daily he logged on but there was never an email from her. As he knew she would, she was keeping to her word. For weeks his disappointment was like a daily flagellation – and sometimes more than once a day. It became as if he needed a fix of rejection – not to give him a high, but a low, to have a visible confirmation. He could not question or criticise her motives. He approved them. She loved her husband with a depth of feeling and shared experience he could never compete with. Her whole life was there in Swansea – all its networks and ties. All he wanted was some acknowledgement from her that her feelings for him were still there but had had to be put away, that he was not an aberration.

Living alone gave him too much time to think. No matter how he organised his day with lists of jobs, creating rigid timetables of coffee and tea, cleaning the house, tidying the garden, visits to his RSPB group and to the school governing body – always Branwen was in his head.

In time he decided that, far from trying to get rid of her, far from moving on, he should do the opposite: celebrate her. Like those Tour de France cyclists who learned to relish and live in the pain they suffered rather than fight it. He gradually came to see himself not as a victim but a survivor. Loving Branwen had helped him find the best part of himself, he had found a constancy he had not experienced before. That is what he must preserve. *Love is not love that alters when it alteration finds.* It became his creed. So he developed the strength of a new authenticity. His memories and feelings for her he wrapped in red velvet and placed lovingly in a small, polished, carved mahogany box in a section of his mind. Had Branwen done the same? He enjoyed the picture of himself as a medieval knight, bearer of courtly love. It was an image he liked, it had a nobility and grace.

★

What bloody nonsense! What a total prat I was, I am! A foolish, foolish old man. He wondered how she explained it all to herself now, years later, and how she would in the future as an old lady, reminiscing. Would she be as harsh as she had been in Manchester, would time have dimmed her memories or softened them?

It was during those months of no contact that he began to construct fictions: imaginary snatched weekends away with Branwen, the eventual restoration of contact which then became a long and loving epistolary relationship – a literary affair of rare beauty, even – far into the future when he and Hugh were dead – Branwen alone of a winter evening, musing, glad she had experienced this strange, alluring richness of love for him and glad that she had managed it so that no one had been hurt. He would not be there to know it, so he had to imagine it. He displaced her rejection of him.

Stop it! For Christ's sake stop it! Forever going round my head.

Jack's circular walk has brought him back to the churchyard now. The mist had thinned and now there is a brief gleam of sun from a broken sky. Turning his face to catch the warmth, he feels the hunched earth relax and turn its body to the sun after the lashing storm.

He phones for the taxi, which would pick him up in thirty minutes, time in which to brood, clean his boots in the wet

121

grass, pick up a stick and throw it violently into the river, watch it swirl away. He wishes he had not sent his last message to her, about going to Bardsey. *It was finished. Grow up, like her – it's not too late.*

5. WALK, DAY FIVE

Jack sits in the public toilet shed at the National Trust car park at Porth Oer. It is a clean, neat place, well kept and newly painted for the season. The car park was empty when the taxi dropped him off so he is probably the first user of the day. As he sits with his trousers round his calves, tucked into thick walking socks, he feels at peace with himself – the deep-seated pleasure of releasing tension, unburdening himself, his familiar, comforting, intimate smell rising from the bowl. Aromatherapy.

So he sits in post-evacuation pleasure, leaning slightly forward, elbows on his thighs, a slight movement of air through the shed freshening his bared buttocks, his lower abdomen area feeling lighter. He notices a small vase of flowers on the windowsill. He stretches up to touch them with his fingers to check they are not plastic. They are fresh daffodils. *A civilised touch.*

Another source of Jack's pleasure is the knowledge that this is his last day of walking and that he will enjoy it. The sun is shining, there is a breeze, and he will revisit places he knows well. Half his project will have been completed. His knees have not failed him, his heart's rhythm has caused him no concern. He thinks of the heightened excitement of the medieval pilgrims as they too set out on the last day of their trek: hardened foot soles or worn shoes padding along, wooden staves tapping out the final miles, prayers chanted, voices louder in anticipation, laughter at the end in sight. They were believers, certain about the holy island. For a time they would forget the dangers of crossing Bardsey Sound, the last barrier.

Jack pulls up and belts his trousers, flushes the toilet, washes his hands, slings his rucksack back on and takes his trekking pole from the corner. First he takes the steep track down to the beach. His father brought him here sixty years ago, his father revisiting his own boyhood holiday scenes from forty years before that. The beach is known as Whistling Sands and his father had explained to him why: as the grains of sand are pressed together by a bare foot, they emit a squeaking or whistling sound. Jack remembers as a child walking along the dry sand to experience it for himself, then telling his father he heard nothing. This early morning in his boots Jack tries it again and there is a sound, a faint whistle for each footstep. Fleetingly he wishes Branwen were there to hear it and make her footsteps beside his, holding hands, leaning into each other. *A century ago my father stepped here in the same way, his footprints are long gone.* Jack turns and walks back, noticing his own footprints already eliding into the level sand, the breeze flicking increments of dry grains into the indentations.

He passes the shuttered café and back up on the cliff top he looks down at the jagged black rocks where he had watched his grandsons crabbing last summer, in their wetsuits on a cold day, angling their nets and tipping the caught crab into a bucket. As a boy Jack had spent hours engineering sand roads along the rock sides, using lolly sticks to create bridges over tiny pools of water caught on the ledges or to shore up embankments, pushing his dinky lorries up the roads. His grandsons hadn't been interested as he showed them how to do it. They had run to new companions among the crab pools.

He turns away and follows a green track past a double fence, up a steep set of steps, zigzagging to a gate. Beyond this, the path descends to a bridge over a stream then contours along the coast past two small tidal islands. White clouds briefly obscure the sun, their shadows hurrying across the hill of Mynydd Carreg. According to the map, the path rises past hut circles but Jack sees no sign of them. As the path bends round the side of Mynydd Anelog, Bardsey Island suddenly comes into sight: that familiar whale back shape, black against the sea. Jack stops and leans on his pole: the end of his journey, the goal of the pilgrims. Doubtless they would have dropped to their knees in thanksgiving, their faith confirmed. Jack feels only ambivalence: the planned end is in sight, within reach, but does he have faith in himself? His mission is suddenly made real: the finality of his impending decision. Yet how he has been loving life these last few days.

Sentiment. Ego. Cowardice.

He shakes his head and gives a wry, weary smile. Past cottages and farms, along green tracks through blazing yellow gorse, he ascends the last rise of Mynydd Mawr, the Land's End of Wales. On the top, just below the old coast guard station and away from the three cars parked at the end of the concrete track, he takes off his rucksack and sits down. He can see the whole shape of the island now, even a building or two on the westward-facing flat land. He looks down at the swirling currents and eddies, the curls of white waves. No wonder the Welsh named it Ynys Enlli, the Island of the Tides. He leans back against the grassy slope and closes his eyes, the breeze here stronger and tousling his hair. Fragments of memories: grandfather with his bow legs and long khaki shorts levering himself out of his old Rover that he has coaxed up the rough track; his father leaning on his stick, looking out to Bardsey, doubtless with his own childhood memories; his mother terrified of him on the steep cliffs; Abi and Tom running in the wind and then having sandwiches in the campervan as it rocked in the gale; Kathy and Megan helpless with laughter as they watched him being chased across a field by a randy, cantankerous goat, him desperately stumbling over a stone wall to safety then clambering with him down the path to St Mary's Well; Branwen stooping to drink the pure water from

125

the well, kissing him with her cool, wet lips. All here in this place; brimful.

And so to Branwen, the last act.

★

For a full year after her farewell at the Lowry Centre there had been no contact between them. Then one afternoon in April when the rain and wind beat at his home, Jack broke his silence and his resignation. In a burst of pent-up intensity he emailed her that, in a month or so, he would be travelling to Skomer Island, near St David's, to birdwatch. Could he meet her for coffee on his way through Swansea? He pressed the 'Send' button with a wild excitement, having allowed his need to break the rules. But he slumped again over the following days as no response came. Then one morning there was a new email.

> *Yes, that would be nice. Tell me day and time and we could meet in Kardomah Café.*
> *Branwen.*

His heart sang as it once had – a ludicrous overreaction on his part, as if she had reached out and touched him. How desperate he must be for acknowledgement that he was still in her life, albeit hidden away in a recess with old dusters and out-of-date bottles of sherry. Perhaps now – distanced by time and fortified by the period of non-communication, grounded again in her marriage – she was able to accept into her head the reality of what they had rekindled, without it being a threat. But when he calmed down and reread the message he saw it was devoid of emotion – *nice!* It was to the point, no kisses.

He wondered why she had agreed. It was too fanciful even for his fictional scenarios for her to want to start again.

126

Pondering it over the next few days he came to the dismal conclusion that she was wanting to confirm something to herself: that she was 'over' it, firmly in control, definitely at a distance. She would look at him and talk to him and there would be not a single spark of the fire that had blazed between them.

So it was, a fortnight after her email reply, that Jack parked his car at the St David's Shopping Centre and found the Kardomah coffee shop a few streets away. He was deliberately early. As soon as he entered, his fears were confirmed: this was not the place anyone would choose for a private or intimate or romantic meeting. The tables were set in straight lines, quite close together. There were no hidden corners; it was all out in the open. The best he could do was choose a table for two in a corner underneath a gleaming copper wall sculpture of a coffee gatherer pouring a sackful of beans over his feet. It seemed vaguely portentous. He sat with his back to the door so he would not be continually looking up for her arrival, ordered a decaf from the waitress and opened his newspaper. It was a decent, functional place, sort of old-fashioned: several hat and coat-stands, waitresses all in black and mostly older women, the table tops made of Formica with a pattern of black and white coffee beans. There were a few people in and pleasant chatter, no 'musak', which was a blessing.

But a few minutes after he settled down a man came and sat at the table next to him and opened his Telegraph. Jack was angry. He needed some privacy to say what he had rehearsed. There were so many other empty tables. Had Hugh sent a chaperone to eavesdrop? The idea was ludicrous but he still remained conscious of the man whose head was now hidden inside his opened newspaper. He watched an old man come in, pushing a Zimmer with a seat built into it. He carefully hung his coat and yellow scarf on a stand. From a box under his Zimmer seat he took a blue and white striped apron, looped the neck over his head and tied the strings. Then he sat down. A waitress greeted him warmly. He must be a regular, thought Jack.

"The usual?" she asked. He smiled and nodded.

"Coffee and a fish finger sandwich, please."

Then there was a tap on Jack's shoulder. He turned and there she was. Branwen leaned down and kissed him on the lips. She hung up her coat. Stunned by her kiss, nonplussed as to what it meant, Jack watched her, that posture he knew so well, her slender figure, her air of prosperity. How immediately he was responding to the reality of her, all his fictional compensation swept away. She came and sat opposite him.

"I'll order a coffee," she said. "Do you want another?"

He nodded.

"And how are you?" she asked. "Still a keen birdwatcher to travel all this way."

In the past he would have known this was a mischievous, ironic remark. But this time there was no hint of a smile or of laughter in her eyes. What he had rehearsed seemed absurdly out of time and place. They talked, of course, about his birding, about the rag-rugging she had got interested in and the piano playing she was taking up again. The man next to them noisily turned the pages of his paper. Then Branwen looked up and suddenly beamed her marvellous smile, but it was aimed at a man standing behind him. She introduced him as a friend. Jack remained sitting at the table. Branwen and the man stood and seemed to talk for ages, animated and laughing. Was this man more than a friend? Was this another part of the set-up, firmly putting him in his place? He admired and resented her social skills as she switched modes like a public relations professional.

"I'm ordering refills," he said in desperation. She nodded.

He sought out a waitress near the kitchen door and when he returned Branwen was on her own again, the joy in her face gone. They spoke of grandchildren but all the time he was looking at her face for clues as to the meaning of this meeting. All he sensed was that she was assessing her own reaction to him, quietly satisfied that he no longer meant anything to her. Gradually the pauses in the conversation grew longer; he had not the heart to play this role any more or the courage to say what he had wanted to say.

After one of those pauses she leaned closer to him and said softly: "After those thirty years since we broke up, when I had never thought about you and, let's be honest, you had never thought about me – you suddenly came back."

So she too had rehearsed her piece.

"When I was young," she continued, "you were a sort of god to me. Don't deride me. It was true. Your idealism, your energy, how different you were to anyone I had ever known. And then you came back into my life, seeking forgiveness. Yes, the memories came back and the old passion. Perhaps it was my mid-life crisis. You arrived and the life I was happily living seemed too neat and orderly and organised, set to run smoothly to the end. You jolted me, for a long time."

She paused for a moment to take a sip of coffee.

"I tried to put an end to it several times, but each time I was drawn back to you. Yes, I had real feelings again for you, they were genuine. There was nostalgia, too. Yes, it was a renewed excitement I was reluctant to set aside. It made me feel good: that was the flattery. You know I'm vain. Then at last I came to my senses, realised what I was putting into jeopardy: all the good things, the solid, meaningful things. I could not live my deception any longer."

She paused. Somewhere in his head were the scattered words of what he had wanted to say. But it was hopeless now. She took a last drink of coffee and suddenly stood up.

"I'm sorry but it has to be this way. I will never see you again. I will never communicate with you again."

She took her coat and tapped his shoulder lightly as she walked past him. He sat there, his shoulder burning with her touch. He had never felt so desolate. Once before, he had suggested he was only an aberration in her life. She had denied it. Now he wasn't just an aberration, he was an irrelevance. He heard the man turn the pages of his Telegraph.

She had kept her word: over the next eighteen months there was no communication. Jack returned to his fictional world and kept the faith of his feelings for her. Then, unable to resist, he sent her a book recommendation for her reading group. She thanked him politely but added only that she and Hugh had just returned from a cruise to celebrate their wedding anniversary. Jack took the hint. He burned with humiliating embarrassment that he had once emailed her, long ago, begging her to attend his funeral, needing to know that she would be at the back of the church, her presence a confirmation of all they had felt for each other. So much pathetic romantic nonsense; no fool like an old fool. Their emailing had again ceased and there had been no further contact until he texted her that he was on this pilgrimage among their old haunts.

★

Jack opens his eyes, feels the breeze light on his face. *What a crazy life!* Yet, after all his other failures, he had achieved a kind of constancy, albeit sleeved in fantasy. *Perhaps that's all I'm capable of.* He looks down over the small stone-walled fields. *That must be the hut.* It is a small, low, wooden building in the corner of a field, the place where a nun lived alone for twenty-five years. She left only three years ago. He had read her book, about her life of simplicity and giving thanks to God: only a different kind of fantasy. It was a way of life he could not understand: the implied concept of a God who wanted someone to be constantly grateful to him; the assumption that she, the nun, mattered that much to him that her prayers were noted and appreciated. *The self-centredness, the self-importance.* Yet it was the opposite she had intended.

Had the nun's life been more worthwhile than his? For all his inadequacies and failures, he cannot believe it. He had muddied the waters, he had tried. If a God had created his complexity, given him his good and bad qualities, at least he had tried to do things with them. God or no God, he had at least improved the human gene pool: his kids had grown into better human beings than he had. Wasn't that the point of evolution? He had fulfilled his primary purpose. Of course he himself is a joke – as much of a joke, at least, as the nun or the hymn-singers or the communicants.

Joke? Potsherd? Immortal diamond? Joke was nearest the mark. He could not see himself as immortal diamond. *Except in the sense of recycled carbon, my atoms along with beer bottles, cardboard, newspapers and plastic coleslaw tubs. In the great green wheelie-bin, awaiting collection.*

Now for the last lap. His knees creak as he stands up, having to twist his torso round, using his arms to push himself up. *Nearly fifty miles done. Not bad! The kids better be damn well impressed with that when they read his note, the one he will leave on the cottage table.*

He slings on his rucksack, bends to pick up his pole, straightens up and sets off. At the top of the gully that leads down to St Mary's Well, he pauses. He should visit it again, complete the cycle. Twice a day the tide covers it yet it soon flows pure again. The old pilgrims drank from it as the waves slopped into the gully below them and the coracles bobbed and swayed. His knees really don't want to climb down to it, it would be painful. No, he will keep as his last memory of it his visit with Branwen: the waves rough and grey, breaking up the rock, the path slippery, Branwen kissing him and transferring her mouth-warmed spring water to his mouth for him to swallow. *When everything seemed possible and life was rich.*

He walks on, over stiles, up slopes of moorland, around fenced fields full of cattle, rounding the final headland into Aberdaron Bay. Traversing the cliffs Jack sees red lobster pots in the water below, the remains of a stone quay. Then painfully, slowly, he descends the steep steps to Porth Meudwy, one of the embarkation points for the medieval pilgrims and where, tomorrow, Jack will follow them. A small boat is on the water, roped to a buoy. A bearded man in a thick jersey is fiddling with the engine of a tractor. He does not look up as Jack passes. Lobster pots are stacked up by a small concrete shed. There's an odd, square-looking, yellow metal boat on a trailer on the slipway. Jack climbs the steep steps up the other side. At the top, the village of Aberdaron is clear to see, dogs and kids running on the beach, small family parties sheltering behind windbreaks. The path follows the cliff top then descends steeply to the beach and Jack is soon crossing the sand and the outlet of a stream before reaching the sea wall. He sits down on a bench, perched on the edge so he doesn't have to take off his rucksack. Now he has reached his journey's end, he is not fatigued.

Done it! He grins. *Didn't think I would. Bound to be something to go wrong. But it didn't. Amazing!*

He texts Megan and Abi and Tom: 'Success!' He wants his kids to be proud of him. Is that natural or childish, he wonders? A dog is barking as it rushes into the sea after a thrown stick. Behind a windbreak a woman is pouring coffee from a flask. A boy, with his father standing nearby, is flying a kite. It bucks and swerves in the wind. In a black wetsuit a young girl is riding the waves on a bodyboard. Jack looks at his watch: 16:23. From the sand he picks up what looks like a piece of creamy sponge – a dog whelk egg-case: the last of his pilgrimage's daily tokens. Time to book into the hotel, check that his food supplies for the island he ordered from the Pwllheli supermarket have arrived, then a visit to the final church on the route, a shower, dinner, his last hotel sleep, his last Welsh breakfast – and then the voyage across the Sound. Satisfaction.

Twenty minutes later, having dumped his stuff in his room and splashed some cold water on his face, Jack stands on the sea wall, which is all there is between the sea and the churchyard. Before the wall was built it would have bordered the shingle beach itself. On a gravestone he reads: 'There is no death while memory lives.'

True, but memory lives for only three generations – if you're lucky.

He goes inside, waits for his eyes to adjust to the dimmer light, smells the dampness in the stone. He finds the two sixth-century stone monuments to Christian saints and monks. 'Veracius priest lies here,' says one. 'Senecus priest lies here with many brethren,' says the other.

He turns the pages of the visitors' book. 'This place helped me when I was lost.' 'This is a special place.' 'Be hopeful, be expectant. Drive safely, otherwise take risks.' *Spot-on advice but he should have added more: 'Prepare to be disappointed.'*

There is another book in which visitors are invited to write names if they want them remembered in prayers. 'The name will be said aloud and the person concerned simply held to the presence of God.' *I like that: 'simply held to the presence'. No complications, no response assumed. Humility.* He reads through the names and reasons. 'Bravely fighting cancer,' is the most common. 'For healing in their marriage.' There have been early deaths 'into the care of Jesus.' The reasons are statements of absence, thanks and suffering. They are pleas for help. A sob rises into Jack's throat, his eyes water. These honest supplications for the sake of others are laid out in public as if they are unclothed, frail and unprotected – but unafraid of scorn. *I envy them.*

He closes the page and turns away to look at a pebble cairn in the chancel. They are mostly grey slate and have names written on them in thick black pen. Are these like Buddhist prayer flags or mani stones? Are these names of people for whom others have offered prayers? His eyes flicker over the names then stop abruptly. Clearly on one near the top of the pile is written 'Jack Richards'. *Coincidence? It's not an uncommon name.* He looks round quickly at the silent, empty church, as if someone were watching him from behind a pillar. He is uneasy, for a moment imagines a presence in the dusty air. He glances at the crucifix on the altar, a metallic gleam of yellow light. Nothing. Then the latch of the heavy door clangs and echoes. He swings round. Nothing again. *Don't be ridiculous; it must be coincidence. That's what coincidences are: unlikely connections. Omen? No, simply happenstance. But it's weird.* He sits down on a chair, one of those placed in a circle instead of the usual rows. *A nice touch, democratic – or is it just because there is such a small congregation? If the pebble really was for me, who could have written it? Who would care enough?* He can think of only three – his children. And they are not believers. *Three! Is that the sum total of people close to me, who really care? And Branwen? Branwen – maybe once, certainly once. But not now. I have disconnected myself, learned to avoid involvement, preferring only superficial contacts.*

Like his mother he had been without a mate, she for thirty-four years, he for only nine. He had tried a couple of meaningless dates from an online dating agency, each time nonplussed as to why he was there, wishing it were Branwen drinking with him, feeling he was sullying his feelings for her. If he had come to realise anything – understand was too strong a word – it was that sanity and safety lay not in the expectation of happiness. The possibility of stoic equanimity was the best he could hope for.

During those nine years he had felt himself gradually, painlessly, detaching from everything – people, pleasure, aspiration – sliding away. Moments of pure pleasure still happened to him: brief connections with his children in phone calls, the lovely periods when Megan was home from university, watching the beauty of Spain's football, the visible approach down the valley of a shower of rain, the patterns of water in a stream, a blackbird on the bird table, the sun breaking through morning mist, reading words that took his breath away with their perception. He knew he could find such moments in music, too, but they would create emotions that would overwhelm him, hurt him with their intensity. So he never listened although he had racks of CDs that were mementos of his life. He remembered episodes of Kathy's life that scythed through him with their immediacy, made him sob and howl in the night: their wedding reception at their home, Kathy so attentive to Abi and Tom, bringing them into the centre, embracing them into her own happiness, flashing to him through the mêlée of guests looks of pure love and the mischievous promise of uninhibited passion.

But this detachment had not been deliberate. A woman's body naturally prepares itself during pregnancy for the life it will shortly create, then, after the reproductive process ceases, it dries up. Perhaps the mind too instinctively prepares itself for death: beginning to tire, forget, content to stare into space and doze, unworried by confusion, no longer exasperated by not hearing properly. His detachment, too, had been a natural evolution.

If he didn't laugh he would cry: see it all as comedy, even absurdity, not tragedy. After all, his life signified nothing. That was what he had to remember. Then he could rest more easily, laugh at the exertions and hopes of his younger life, the fantasy of his dotage.

He had watched Le Tour de France on TV as a parable: long, flat stretches, category climbs, time trials, sprint finishes, cobbles, crashes and punctures, endurance, drugs and doping and – for a few, occasionally – the podium moments. And the utter pointlessness of this noble striving? Not quite, for there will be for a time a memory, a name on a record, but only to be lost in an archive, replaced by the next name.

And my own scorecard – the one I've been keeping all week? What a fatuous idea! Think back and assess – but what are the criteria for success? Regret and guilt – do I excuse myself or approve myself or condemn myself? What could I have done better? You leave only your reputation – and that's too strong a word, maybe an anecdote or two mentioned sentimentally at family gatherings once a year. Growing old ungracefully, dropping tissues out of your pocket, needing to pee in the hedgerows, writing lists because the brain cells are already shuffling off this mortal coil. They know the score. How did I score myself? Eighteen out of forty, I think. Bloody typical – just below average, not good enough, room for improvement. And that's being generous. Branwen I've left out of the calculation. She's beyond arithmetic.

From his pocket he takes out the wooden dodecahedron. He had read that it represents the ether, the essence, God if you like, the universe, the zodiac. His fingers stroke its fine-grained sides of twelve regular pentagons. *This church is the place for it, I suppose, full of prayers. And all the while the Earth turns and erodes, the galaxies fly apart, stars are born and die.*

Subdued by these thoughts, he stands up. He is hungry now and he uses this to push away an incipient sadness. *Branwen.* He pushes her away too as he closes the church door behind him and smells the sea breeze, feels it fresh on his face.

After an early dinner, too early to sit in his room on the top floor, its window looking out onto a slate roof, he sits on the window seat at the back of the bar with his half pint of orange and soda. The bar is packed with families, foursomes of young people, retired couples – all making their choices from the menus.

"May we join you?"

It's a couple who had been having their meal in the corner of the dining room, he'd noticed their frequent bursts of laughter.

"Of course," said Jack, making a bit more room.

"Bit of a crush in here," says the man, squeezing in.

"But you like a crush, don't you, love?" giggles the woman, squeezing herself in beside him.

He has a pint of bitter, she a gin. *In their late fifties? Second marriage? Too jovial to be a long-married couple. Both short and overweight.*

"Here for the weekend?" asks the man. "Oh, I'm Peter and this is Linda."

They shake hands, Linda leaning round Peter, revealing her ample, pale, soft bosom. Jack explains his godless pilgrimage and that he's going to Bardsey next day.

"I'm glad you said godless," says Peter. "We're here for a dirty weekend, aren't we, my love?" And they both shake with laughter.

So, unasked, they tell their tale. Peter is a postman, living in a small north Midlands village near to an Evangelical Divinity College. His wife died two years ago. Linda is a civil servant clerk and lives in Shrewsbury with five grown-up children from two previous marriages. As they talk in tandem Jack watches them. He sees Peter's almost-bald head, his glasses, belt tight under his paunch, his thick wrists. Linda has a fat face – no other word for it – and short black hair and bright gold earrings, bright lipstick, chubby cheeks. Her forearms, like her bosom, are freckled, her fingers short and stubby. *How I hate short fat fingers on women. Must be something sexual about that. Who was that comedian who said he preferred a woman to have short fingers because it made his prick look longer?*

"We came here for our first weekend together, didn't we, Peter? We came in separate cars."

"Very romantic, and here we are again," laughs Peter. "Can't keep away!"

Jack notices there's a gold stud in the man's left ear.

"Do you mind me asking," he says, "but isn't it painful getting your ear pierced?"

137

"It was me. I asked him to do it," laughs Linda. "Told him he had to break out a bit."

Peter lives in a close, a sort of cul-de-sac, in an ordinary semi on an estate of private houses.

"I love it," he says, "when Linda arrives on a Friday evening and parks her car in the driveway. Most of the neighbours are connected with the college, still spouting fire and brimstone. And Linda walks up the door, rings the bell and waits, looking round. We know they're all looking, the neighbours."

Peter chuckles again.

"We're the talk of the village," says Linda, and she laughs too, wobbling. *Too fleshy for me.* "I love being the new woman and that we're not married."

"Seize the moment," says Peter. "Carpe diem. Doesn't it say that in the Bible?"

Jack sees him hold Linda's fleshy arm and stroke it with his short fat fingers.

"We always have a stroll along the beach before we go to bed," says Peter.

"I love the waves rolling in, in the dark," adds Linda, finishing her drink. "Time for that, Peter, before it's too late. Nice talking to you."

Shoving their generous bums along the seat, they manoeuvre their way out. How Megan would have enjoyed the conversation. Jack feels suddenly deflated, the air around him flat and uncharged. *They don't look the part but, by God, they're actually doing it. Living it. It's real. Real bodies touching. Being together. Their eyes sparkle when they look at each other. So uncomplicated, direct. Loving their roles. It's as open as those prayer pleas in the church, but the opposite: having fun not beseeching. They look nondescript but they are being bold and merry.*

He takes a long drink of his orange, drains the glass.

And I just live a fucking fiction, an unrequited, courtly fucking love. Branwen, I want us slipping on the shingle, holding hands, tasting the salt in the air, hearing the waves breaking. I want to make love with you, abandoned, shameless, like we used to do. We lived then. Not slouching to death.

A sudden spasm of hate for her, and then it was gone.

What he wanted to remember was the intense sensitivity Branwen and Kathy, in their separate times, had bestowed upon him, a state of acute receptiveness in which memories of her led him to seek immediate sensual delights. That far distant late summer day he can recall with cruel clarity. He had pitted green olives for lunch. Inside his mouth he pressed an olive up against the back of his teeth with his tongue and sucked out the slightly sharp taste, which he then felt at the back of his throat. He felt the flesh of the olive slowly dissolve. He went out into the garden to collect the last of the raspberry crop. He took off his sandals and rolled up the bottoms of his trousers. The air was warm and still, the garden stream gently descending and fresh. The flat stepping stones were warm and smooth to his soles, the lawn still damp from the night rain, grass blades wet between his toes, the lawn giving and soft beneath his heels, fallen copper beech leaves brittle against his ankle bones. He sought underneath the drenched leaves for the hidden raspberries on bending canes, the fine-thorned stems scratching him – delighted as his skin came alive. With just the right pressure between his fingers he eased off each raspberry whole, leaving the small cone-shaped plug creamy and exposed, inviting. His fingers were stained red with juice, which he licked off. He was half crazy with this intensity.

From deep down, he surfaces into the boisterous chatter of the bar and looks around, disorientated. *In what way am I part of this?* Slowly, steadily, he climbs the stairs to his room. He rests on the landing. *I have lived, after all. Not long till resolution.*

139

6. BARDSEY

Plastic sacks of coarse grit and sheep food are being passed up from the trailer to the boat. Jack stands on the narrow slipway and watches. It is all so workaday. A couple of young birders are also going to the island, he with wild curly hair, his girl a sleek blonde, to stay at the observatory. They are loading several large white tubs labelled 'obs'. The boatman stacks all the stuff into the small wheelhouse on the bright yellow steel twin-hulled boat. Jack anxiously checks that his bags and parcels of foodstuffs are on board. Each package has had to be wrapped in waterproof sheeting and bound with parcel tape.

The departure is too mundane, thinks Jack. Was it like this also in medieval times when the pilgrims came here – the Hermits' Port – to complete their pilgrimage, or even earlier back in the sixth century when, from the tip of the headland, monks and hermits clambered into skin-covered coracles? Is it just business to the locals, earning a living from the holy island across the Sound, scoffing at the incompetence of the landsmen? The pilgrims and monks were travelling to the edge of the world, seeking some kind of resurrection or even a grave. Now it is his turn. Godless pilgrim though he is, he is travelling towards a decision, a conclusion. Chattering, relaying the luggage, none of his fellow travellers will guess his purpose as he stands there in his boots and over-trousers, his woolly cap and layers of fleece and jacket, composing camera shots: the red tractor and trailer, the yellow boat on its trolley, the green swell surging into the narrow inlet between black rocks. Even as he takes the photos of this final part of his odyssey, he wonders why. For whom will they be a record?

"OK, ladies and gentlemen," announces the boatman in his lilting Welsh accent, his thin hair blowing in the breeze, brown eyes bright, face weather-beaten. So they climb the rickety ladder between the huge outboard motors onto the open deck. There is cover for the luggage but not for passengers.

"Life jackets please."

They pull the bulky orange contraptions over their heads, tie the long black tapes and select their places on metal benches along the sides or on a wooden box in the middle. The birders have already got their places in the lee of the wheelhouse. The tractor pushes the boat trolley into the water. Alun the boatman waves his hand when it floats and the tractor returns with the trolley up the slipway. The boat reverses out into the black water, turns, accelerates and speeds along the headland, close into the rocks where the sheltered water is calm. Jack looks back to Aberdaron, the first time he has seen it from the sea, the church low beside the beach, the wide bay of Hell's Mouth stretching east. Was it sixty years ago when he had first run on that beach, bathed in the cold sea?

Then they round the headland and Bardsey appears, its mountain like a great whale back. The sea changes: there are white breakers everywhere, the boat bouncing into the waves and the troughs between them. Spray breaks on either side of the boat. Jack realises he's chosen the wrong side, the one he now sees has the tide race running into it. Gripping the gunwhales, he is drenched, his hood pulled over his head. He looks back at Uwchmynydd, sees the track down to St Mary's Well. He'd not gone there yesterday, tired towards the end of his week's walk.

"I'll slow down," yells Alun. Jack looks out at the currents and whirlpools. How did those coracles cross? No wonder the Pope decreed that three pilgrimages to Bardsey equalled one to Rome. He looks for the nun's wooden cabin up on the headland.

Soon they are in the lee of the island, speeding up along the shore of black rock pierced by gullies and caves, guillemots nesting on the ledges. The boat slows again as they round a rock outcrop and come into a small bay, the red and white lighthouse, its light flashing even during the day out at the southern end of the island. The tide is in and there are dozens of sleek black seal heads poking out of the green water, observing them. This is Y Cafn: the landing place, the haven. Alun steers the boat onto the trailer, leaps out in his waist-high boots, jumps onto the tractor and hauls the boat up the slipway. Unloading begins immediately while the passengers disembark. How often Jack has looked across the Sound at this island and now, at last, he stands on it – next to piles of lobster pots, an old broken black boat, a bright steel yellow landing craft, ugly and squared off, and a stack of red and white tubs of 'Ewe-master, mineral lick for all sheep'.

The island steward, introducing himself as Rhys, points out to Jack where he is staying.

"That low grey farm building with the green door. I'll be with you in a couple of minutes."

So Jack goes up the track that curves below the hill, past the white-painted farmhouse, which is now the bird observatory, and turns in at a farm gate. A path has been mown through the long grass to a small slate-flagged terrace with two white wrought-iron chairs that sit outside his green door. Jack turns to look at the view: south-west to Argentina, he had read somewhere, down across sheep and lamb-filled fields to the narrows where the landing place is, and beyond to where the green southern half of the island broadens out with the lighthouse and its white buildings. All around the black-rocked coast the sea is white with breaking waves.

He opens the top half of the green stable door, unbolts the bottom half and steps inside. It feels colder inside than out, a stone-flagged floor, the walls of stone painted white, a big, plain table with a vase of fresh flowers, two wicker armchairs, an open wooden staircase in one corner. There is one small window, looking south. He goes up and looks in the loft bedroom: two single beds, with a pair of brown blankets folded on each, either side of a small table under the window, two old chests of drawers.

"Are you there?" calls a voice from downstairs.

Jack goes down.

"It's your first visit," says Rhys, "so you'll need a bit of Health and Safety."

He explains about the gas camping lamp, the Calor gas-fired heater, the stove and fridge.

"Oh and there's no locks on the cottage doors. But don't worry. None of us have locks on the doors. And the only people on the island are three birding assistants, me, and the farmer's family. That's all there are this week. It's before the season, you see. And there's the toilets."

There is one in the old pigsty adjoining the cottage, chemical, which Jack will have to empty at the end of the week.

"Just chuck on a handful of sawdust every time you use it. Or there's the public toilets which happen to be in your back yard and which you won't have to empty. I'll show you."

In a wooden shed across the yard is the Twin Full Access Composting Toilet with a poster that explains how it worked. They go back into the cottage, which Jack now sees is just a section of the byres and sties of the old farm.

"Come to me if you need any help. Read that form and sign it and I'll collect it. They'll leave your luggage at the gate. Oh, and use the filtered water to brush your teeth."

Rhys explains about filling the bucket with rainwater from the tank to do washing, then putters off up the track in his 4x4 buggy. While Jack is pottering around the cottage, reading the welcome pack and putting on a kettle of well water to boil,

143

the farmer deposits the luggage from his tractor trailer, gives a friendly wave and also disappears up the track. It doesn't take Jack long to unroll his sleeping bag, augmented with the fleece blanket he'd put in at the last minute, and pack away his clothes and the food.

He makes his coffee and sits in the sun, glad for the warmth after the chilly interior. The view is lovely, the silence after the tractor engine fades broken only by the bleat of lambs in the field beyond his wall. This is his sought-after peace. He looks up at the mountain, Mynydd Enlli. *The island had turned its back on the mainland.* He loves that description, it is so true: none of where he is can be seen from the mainland. It is a kind of hermitage, not a solitary one but a private one. He had loved the idea of being here, sitting under a blue sky. He should be content. Austerity, he knows, was a pilgrim's tool, and solitariness essential. But already he is feeling not lonely but lonesome – and he is drinking coffee in broad daylight. Crows are calling high up the mountain, and he sees two ravens in the field. 'Branwen', she had told him, meant 'beautiful raven' in Welsh. He watches them, sleek and efficient and beautiful in an intimidating way. Sending that text had been ridiculous. She had not replied.

To hell with this morbidity! He'll wander up to the abbey, see if there is any sense left of this being a holy island. He meets Alun the boatman walking up to the abandoned farm.

"Settled in?" asks Alun.

"Fine, thanks."

Alun points at the ground and scrubs it with the toe of his boot.

"See those two edges of stone, diagonal across the track? It's a thousand-year-old tomb. Skeleton in it. I always make sure I walk round it, but if I drive over it in the tractor I always feel a bit funny. Enjoy the island. I was born on it but just live here during the summer now."

144

He goes on his way and Jack continues up to the tower: all that remains of the thirteenth-century Augustinian abbey. It is only fifteen feet high, roofless. He passes through the gate into the remains of the graveyard – 20,000 had reputedly been buried on the island. Ploughing regularly turned up human bones, he had read. Now there are only a few slate-covered tombs and three huge Celtic crosses, but not ancient ones. One grave is of the lighthouse keeper's wife who had died in childbirth at the age of thirty-two. He goes down the steps to the foot of the tower. There are two rotting wooden pews set by the wall, a slab of slate for an altar. In a gap in the stone wall is another piece of thin slate, pierced through by the carving of a cross. It is gloomy and weeds grow on the stone floor where stone and dirt have accumulated.

Jack wants to feel something. He almost yearns for it: some sense of the past, some remnant in the air of all that prayer and hope.

A serious house on serious earth it is…
Which, he once heard, was proper to grow wise in,
If only that so many dead lie round.

He sits on the corner of a slate-topped tomb, purple and warm in the sun. So many footprints here, so much praise and prayer that have ascended into the air and faded, so many pleas and hopes. For many, he knows, this was a liminal place, a threshold between one reality and another, a place where the veil between this world and the next is at its thinnest. A crossing place. He has no such faith. Religion had been a necessary fiction for those who travelled here from the sixth century on, monks, hermits, pilgrims. Yet he sits here watching and waiting, feeling the warm air move on the breeze. Is he hoping there might yet be a revelation, an epiphany, a consolation? But there is nothing. It is at the same time a disappointment and a confirmation. The sun is still bright but lowering slowly into the west behind the Wicklow mountains across the Celtic Sea. He steps out of the graveyard, latching the gate behind him. Time for something to eat.

He enters the chill and gloom of the cottage. He seems to have a choice: either he leaves the door open so the kitchen is light but cold, or closes the door so that it is gloomy but warming up with the gas heater on. He can't have both light and warmth.

As the evening cools he lights the Camping Gaz lamp and the Calor gas heater and boils his well water to cook some rice, which he eats with a packet of chicken sauce at the empty table. He fills up the bucket from the rainwater tank and washes the dishes. In the wicker chair he reads, hears the farmer's quad bike pass along the track, watches the light fade from the window. Then the lamp runs out of Gaz, and the heater cuts out every time he tries it on maximum. In thermal T-shirt, padded shirt and fleece, he tries to read by torchlight but it gives no pleasure. So he brushes his teeth in filtered water and goes up to bed. The bedroom is icy. Keeping his socks on, he wriggles into his sleeping bag, draws up the fleecy blanket, ties the drawstring of the bag tight around his shoulders, finds he cannot read with his head torch because his arms are too cold, gives in and turns off the torch. The silence is intense, the darkness complete except for the lighthouse beam flashing round in its regular pattern.

At three in the morning he has to pee. He struggles out of his bag, puts on his head torch, slips his trekking sandals and his fleece jacket on and pads down the stairs. Shadows loom as he passes the doors to the outhouse and he stands in the dark yard. Looking up, the sky is a litter of glittering stars; it is cold and clear enough for a frost. His head torch flashes its narrow beam around the doors of the old byres, wall corners illuminated and then cast back into darkness. Out in the fields he hears the cackling and caterwauling of thousands of Manx shearwaters as they come under cover of darkness from the sea to their burrows in the old walls and along the mountain. Back in the house he latches the doors, thinks again how vulnerable he is – but to whom on this silent island with only seven other sleepers? In his sleeping bag he luxuriates in warming up, wonders why he must endure this for six more nights. The visit is maybe a big mistake except that he can still think of no better place to conclude matters. Eventually he sleeps.

★

He sleeps well, only waking after it is light. After a cold-water wash and a breakfast of Dorset 'Luscious Berries and Cherries' muesli with long-life milk, Jack makes some instant decaf coffee and leans on the open stable door looking down the island. It is a still, grey day. Pied wagtails are flitting about, landing on the remains of the whim stone by the well just outside the door. Then he hears a repeated high-pitched sound, 'chow, chow'. He looks up and sees a flock of nine black birds circling, swooping and diving. They must be choughs. He watches them land on the field, quickly gets his binoculars and identifies their red legs and curved red beak. The day has got off to a good start.

"There's nothing to do, and all day to do it in," someone has written in the visitors' book. Today he will walk along the western side of the island, taking his camera and his binos. A wind is getting up so he packs his headband into his small rucksack with his over-trousers and a flask of coffee, puts on his fleece and his waterproof jacket, picks up his trekking pole and sets off. He passes three other self-catering houses, all empty, passes the abbey tower and the old farm, climbs over stiles into the fields below the small plantation of wind-bent trees. Spring surrounds him: lambs, first curious about him,

147

then running in panic to their mothers; in the field of Welsh Black cattle only one calf so far, sticking close to its mother; birds busy with nesting material in their mouths; bright yellow gorse everywhere, splodges of bird shit outside the old rabbit burrows and gaps in stone walls where the shearwaters are already nesting. Down on the coast rocks there are oystercatchers and herring gulls, two guillemots swimming near a pink lobster pot. The sea is crashing up the deep gullies.

Jack is seeking what he self-mockingly calls 'intimate landscapes': photos of lichen patches on rocks, rusting iron rings in old wood, rope tied round gates, the herringbone pattern of stones in the old walls. Wedged behind rocks out of the wind, watching the tide ebbing, again he wonders why he is still doing this, so close to his final life–death decision. Habit? To give his walk a purpose? To freeze time for a moment? Because he wants to discover accidental beauty until the end? Perhaps it is a last, sentimental gift to his photographer son who will without doubt examine his camera.

He levers himself up and wanders along the path that follows every indentation and outcrop on the coast. Stepping through a gap in a wall, he almost treads on a rope. It is thick and has been shaped into a heart, worked down into the sheep-cropped turf so it is securely fixed. Someone has fashioned it – a visitor or maybe one of the farmer's family on a still day in the winter when they were the only inhabitants. Is it a statement, a dream, a longing, a farewell? It is a gesture of some kind. The heart shape is empty. It is there to fill with whatever emotion he chooses, or – more accurately – whatever emotion chooses him. This morning, in the greyness and to the sound of the ceaseless sea, it is inevitably melancholy.

He walks on and is soon at the bay of Solfach, once the traditional landing place and the only sandy beach on the island. The wind has grown in strength and Jack is glad to see the small bird hide at the back of the beach, painted black, its roof weighted down with stones. He stoops and steps into the gloom inside, the hide enclosing him in its dark wooden walls. Immediately he feels the relief of being out of the wind. He unbolts the viewing panels, settles down and pours himself a coffee from his flask. In all his gear, it is warm inside, on the wooden bench barely long enough for two people. He gets out his binoculars. Once again, like a hermit, he is watching and waiting.

He has completed his pilgrimage, contemplated his life and has come, without the help of some supernatural being, to a conclusion he knew when he set out: he has failed everyone he is supposed to have loved, but he is convinced he is not a bad man. The world has not disappointed him, nor have other people. His only disappointment is himself. He has been a parasite, sucking nourishment – whether this is intellectual or emotional or experiential – from others. He has depended on clever, educated friends who knew about architecture and the Renaissance, about geology and birds or who have taken him on adventures, climbing sea cliffs in Scotland, snowy arêtes at dawn in the Alps; on women who have loved and encouraged him, borne his children and borne with him. But he himself has been a hollow man. At times he thought he had made decisions about directions in his life. Now he realises these decisions have been made for him by a mixture of random genes and circumstances. Unknowingly, his actions have simply been an unfolding of his own character, a slow but certain distillation of what is at the core of him. This is the only revelation he has experienced: a recognition of himself.

"We are who we are," his mother had once said.

"We live the lives that fit us." Hadn't Branwen said something similar?

Beneath his changing relationships, his opinions and knowledge, there has always lain hidden, like a crab under its shell, the unchanging core of his character. Life isn't about developing character but about its slow exposure – each individual a random mutation, a specific error. He has come to accept who he is – his particular mix of egoism, malice and compassion – but it isn't a cause for celebration.

He has never, or hardly ever, deliberately set out to hurt. Undoubtedly he has hurt but that has been a side effect, not a purpose. And he has been hurt, which helps towards a balance. At times he has even done some good, but it is a side effect, the result of something he's done because he wanted to, a selfish, self-satisfying act. No, he isn't bad, just inadequate. His only consolation is that he probably isn't alone in this.

Now here he is, contemplating another decision. Although he tries to weigh up the pros and cons, the answer is already programmed in his blood. The logic is just a charade. The decision is about another departure – but the final one. All other departures are simply rehearsals for this one – the deaths of parents, of friends, children leaving home, the end of relationships, the decline of muscles and joints, the dribbling away of memories, the fading of the word-hoard, the sagging of enthusiasms. It is all good practice. Time steals everything away before stealing you.

And this is of absolutely no import anyway. It will be as if he has never existed. Why should it be otherwise? *Dust to dust, ashes to ashes* – the Bible has got that right.

He looks out at the small sandy cove. Across the sand, the unseen wind is blowing bits of dried seaweed. He laughs. Perfect. This is the right setting. The tide is ebbing, uncovering glistening seaweed and pebbles. Further out he notices white furrows of waves begin to appear in certain spots, and soon among them dark shapes like the backs of seals but motionless. The shapes become rocks as the tide recedes. About a quarter of a mile out there is a large rock, Carreg Rhona.

In three days' time he will write a brief letter to his children, leave it on the kitchen table in the cottage where Rhys will find it when he comes to collect his luggage, which he will pack properly and label. Also on the table, neatly arranged, will be his five Platonic solids and the five tokens he has collected on each day's walking. Then he will come here while the sand is still covered by the tide so that it will be easier to walk into water. Just as his mother's waters had broken for his birth, now he will break the waters for his death. He will swim towards the north of Carreg Rhona where, if not yet killed by the cold or fatigue or by a heart attack, his body will be swept into the swirling currents and whirlpools and carried off into the Sound. He hopes his body will never be found because he wants no part of him left behind. Branwen will not know nor even think of him. No one will tell her because no one knows she exists. The ridiculous virtual romance that had filled his last decade with such richness and anguish will just be as if it had never existed. He and it will be extinguished together at the same time.

Having formulated his plan, he feels no sense of drama, gives no conclusive sigh, feels no elation or sorrow, not even a final peace. Perhaps he is just exhausted. Shut in this little hut there is no witness to his thoughts or momentous decision – if momentous is the right word. It was just the same as in medieval times. Those pilgrims looked out at the western horizon of their flat world, not noticing the hint of a curve, and saw it as a rim, an edge off which they would drop into… the same nothingness he will drop into. The island is, in the end, a boundary and a threshold – for him as for so many who have preceded him here.

His brain is tired, even becoming bored with these thoughts. He picks up his binos and scans the beach. Up to a dozen pied wagtails flicker and flash along the sand, their legs running so fast they blur like in a cartoon. Redshanks fly across. A pair of shelducks waddle leisurely out from between seaweed-bedraggled rocks, paddle across the bay and take up new stations on rocks on the other side.

Abruptly he puts down his binos. What is he doing? It is ludicrous to be so absorbed and interested: like a condemned man on death row wanting to get to the last chapter of his book and know the resolution before he sits in the electric chair next morning. What is the point? Is it something about the human spirit, about curiosity – all this seeking, this effort to understand? Birds eat, court, make nests, reproduce, nurture their young. It is a clear process: no angst or self-consciousness or questioning their purpose in life. They just live it – skilful, effective, successful, perfectly adapted – and then die. His own usefulness and functionality are over. What had at the time seemed like achievements now seem meaningless. In his career, all of his innovations – argued about, researched, organised – have been replaced, have become outdated and irrelevant. He had wanted to make a difference, had for a time made a difference, a tiny dent in the scheme of things for a few people in a small place but now it is as if he had never passed that way. The way ahead is clear – in a last act of self-discipline he will live the three days before he walks into that cold sea and feels first his feet grow numb. So why is he still identifying birds and being thrilled? He sips his coffee.

And yet walking into the sea, west at sunset towards the rim of the world, what sort of self-important melodrama is that? Looking into that cold green swell, the rolling waves, it could be his final failure. He has a ridiculously low pain threshold. He is a physical coward and walking into that sea will be a physical act. Something deep within him could not believe he would actually do it. Perhaps the answer was to get drunk, the final indignity. He could not even die properly.

Bollocks to it all! *Death is the great opportunity no longer to be me.* He will do it. It fits. He closes up the hide windows and steps outside into the wind and fresh air. Over on the left-hand side of the bay he notices scroll marks in the sand and walks over. There are arabesques and curlicues that someone has drawn with a stick, early this morning as soon as the tide had left the sand clear. Next to the patterns are the words: 'Be of good cheer, I have overcome the world'. Who is this cheerleader? Why this need to evangelise and parade their faith on an empty beach? Is it someone trying to bolster their own beliefs, push out some nagging doubt? Faith is by definition blind, like love.

His eyes have seen both the beauty of the world and the ugliness of himself.

Enough! What Jack wants is a sandwich, another coffee and a Kit Kat in the shelter of some rocks.

★

He wakes at 6.30am, sunlight streaming through the window and the wind, which has blown all night from the north, has abated. It will be a good day for the mountain. After breakfast and the routine of his ablutions – he does not want to scratch his arse in a gorse thicket, his crouching knees trembling with the effort – he packs a picnic and sets off. Easing his way through the gap in the herringbone stone wall, Jack lumbers gracelessly over the stile and starts up the zigzag path. Although he feels fit, he has to go steadily so his heart does not make him breathless. He has to control his ascent, feeling – and no doubt looking – like an old man. But he is going well, picking his way through the bright yellow gorse bushes, snagged with grey sheep's wool, foxglove leaves just pushing through the grass. Then the path levels out onto a small sheltered plateau. He looks for the remains of three Bronze Age hut circles there but cannot find them so pushes on towards the grey crags of the summit rocks. Then he is on the crest looking down the steep drop of the eastern side of the mountain, gulls circling and screaming, a thin, precarious path winding along far below. All around the island, in spite of the lack of wind, the grey-green sea is full of white waves breaking, swirling and surging in contrary directions. Cloud shadows move slowly across the sea, the colour of aubergines, shifting like shoals of fish or floating rafts of seaweed. South-west into the sun, the sea glistens like shot silk. There is no sign of the boat from Aberdaron but a fishing boat bobs between lobster pots.

Into his mind flashes an image of Kathy, on a fishing excursion north of Iceland, just on the Arctic Circle, the Atlantic rough and swollen, himself in the wheelhouse, green and queasy, but Kathy and Megan at the pitching, rolling prow, roaring with laughter in the spray and wildness. There had been great times together.

To the west he can see the silhouette of the Wicklow mountains, to the north snow glints on Snowdonia, to the east curves Cardigan Bay. In front and closer is the Lleyn peninsula, the sun shining on the white cottages scattered over Uchmynydd. He settles down with his back against a rock and with his binos traces the final days of his walk from Yr Eifl down the coast and round Mynydd Anelog – he can just see the white chimneys of the isolated cottages on its sheltered eastern flank. He has walked right along the edge of the brown cliffs in front of him, round the full width of the headland: the heather, small green fields enclosed by stone walls, meandering paths. He looks in silence, sun warm on his face. It is just so beautiful. He feels at peace.

The pilgrims had come to this island looking for a kind of resurrection. He has come, confirming to himself on the beach yesterday, looking for the cul-de-sac of death. But how can he voluntarily cut himself off from all this beauty, how can he abbreviate his only chance of experiencing it? Only a few feet away a skylark stands on a rock with a piece of sheep's wool in its beak. More wagtails are courting. A gang of choughs circles below, calling. He hears the faint bleats of lambs. In the gloomy autumn of his days he is contemplating death while all around him spring is vivacious. He sees Rhys' red 4x4 buggy parked at the lighthouse. He is helping the birder and his girlfriend renovate a stone hut where they will live for the summer. Dressed in white decorating overalls they are climbing ladders onto the roof. Below him at the other end of the island he watches the black cows progress slowly across a field; soon they will be calving. The farmer's tractor silently carries a bale of fodder into the field.

This is a busy island: the farmer and his family; the birders monitoring and numbering shearwater burrows, dating the return of the swallow, spotting the stray woodlark, counting passing gannets; the warden redecorating the self-catering houses and tending his own vegetable plot; visitors soon returning in numbers watching seals, identifying wild flowers or lichen; this year's artist-in-residence arriving; the crab and lobster fishermen increasing. In spite of all the history he has read, in spite of the Celtic crosses in the graveyard and the ruined Augustinian abbey tower and the buried skeletons of the 20,000 Celtic saints, he does not sense the holiness of the place. He had felt a latency at Iona and Lindisfarne, the trace of an energy in the air like incense. Jack knows that Christians still come here occasionally for retreats, to experience some kind of rebirth or reconnection. He regrets the lack, he wants the place to have some kind of aura: its location as well as its history deserves it. It would somehow justify all the efforts medieval people had made to get here. He wants to hear the echo of all their prayers and hopes, to sense the comfort and fulfilment they must have felt. He wants it to be the right place for his own completion. Yesterday in the hide on the beach he had decided on it – but out of a bleakness not a richness.

But no matter how he tries to justify it, it will be a rejection of his children, especially so of Megan – her mother's death and now her father's suicide. How can he even contemplate abandoning her? How would she feel with her father choosing to leave her? What damage would that do to her? He wants to watch her life grow, wants to see her move to the next stage, wants to help her if he can. He looks down below him to the fields and across the Sound to the mainland peninsula, calling choughs circle above the unseen hut circles, bees buzz in the bright gorse and the sun warms his face – here is a real richness. And he is in love with it. Life is brief, with passages of great beauty. How can he cut it short? It will be a betrayal – of the wonder of all this around him, which does not need a god to explain it, of his children and his friends, even of Branwen though she will never know.

Most of all he will be betraying his own life – reflected back at him from the peninsula. Although he has never lived there, it contains all the key stages of his life: playing cricket with his bow-legged grandfather on the beach at Aberdaron; climbing alone to the Giants' Fort on Yr Eifl and wondering about Vortigern and his hidden valley; witnessing the fulfilment of one of his father's dreams when his father had led his whole family down the track to the beach at Tudweiliog, for the first time seeing his father cry, sentimental tears. He has brought Abi and Tom camping many times, on his own in the campervan, watching them throwing the Frisbee while he cooked the tea, sheltering with them under the walls of Criccieth castle as the rain lashed down and the hills of Merioneth disappeared into the mist. He came to St Mary's Well with Kathy and comforted a frightened Megan before going for hot chocolate in Y Gegin where a sign stated the pilgrims of old had taken refreshment. Years after the tragedy of Kathy's death it was on the headland, looking at Bardsey, that he had again walked hand in hand with Branwen, their attraction as electric as before, the impossibilities too great, the potential hurt too overwhelming, the clash of loyalties too stark.

His feelings for Branwen are as strong now as he sits on the summit on Mynydd Enlli. No matter that they are and will remain separate, that she has ceased all communication with him, she still lives warm and smiling in his head. His feelings for her are his saving grace, evidence that he has a goodness and a strength.

Bollocks to moving on – enjoy what you have. Suffering arises from desire, said the Buddhists. Indeed, but that suffering is the core of being human – aspiration, curiosity, always seeking to reach beyond your grasp. In it, like a mineral intrusion in a rock, is richness and latency. Yesterday's conclusion down in the bird hide on the beach was confirmation of what was weak in him and self-pitying; to describe it as a sign of strength was ludicrous, self-denying. His eyes have seen the ugliness in himself but they have also seen the beauty of the world. No, there is still so much to live for, so much still to savour in his head. He shifts his back against the granite. The sun seems to thicken and warm his warfarin-thinned blood, to engorge it with the bright red of life. *Incarnadine,* is that the word? Perhaps after all this is a resurrection of a kind, a renewal born of failure. In all this space – the sky and sea and air and history and legend – he means absolutely nothing. But for an infinitesimal moment in time he is himself, unique, never to be repeated. He hasn't dealt himself the cards, he can only play the hand he's picked up. To sit here like this, to ruminate and yearn, regret and remember, to switch from gloom to elation – well, that is him being himself. His random mix of genes are thriving still, have the same imperatives.

He stands up and slings his daysack on his shoulders, holds his trekking pole. Somehow he wants to salute this place, this vista, praise it, 'hallelujah' it. Before the Augustinian monks with their tonsures and chants, even before the founders, Cadfran and Dyfrig, this place surely had a spiritual significance. An island separated by streaming currents from the end of the headland, its mountain turning it away from the mainland, its hidden fertile land pointing west to the sunset – who could not see it as a boundary, a threshold over which to take a fearful or hopeful step? Jack does not require a god or a set of ceremonies and rites to define that crossing.

He sees the path zigzagging below him. He needs to go slowly, in the right rhythm for his heart, pacing gently for his arthritic knees. Ah, richness! Down by an inlet he will watch the sea birds and eat his sandwich and his dark chocolate Kit Kat.

★

It is midweek and another sunny day, but without the wind. The fatalism by the beach has faded, but so has the elation on the mountain. After an early breakfast, Jack drinks coffee outside, sitting in the sun, which has just spread its warmth over the mountain ridge. He watches the light of the lighthouse circle round in its pattern. He hears the puttering of an engine he could already identify as Rhys' buggy. It halts at the gate.

"Day trippers today," Rhys calls. "Alun's bringing the boat over. It could get crowded."

He waves and is off.

The first boat for four days! In spite of himself, Jack warms to the possibility of human presence, perhaps even a chat. He'll go down to the café. This is actually a shop set up by the farmer's family in a small outhouse with picnic tables set up on a grassy level outside it. He's looked in already, the door always unlocked but with a sign: 'Please close the door so the goat can't get in and eat everything'. It is mostly craft stuff produced by the farmer's family, presumably in the winter months when they are the only people on the island: photographs by the father – seascapes of winter storms and sunsets, and time-lapse shots of star passages across the sky –

and by the son, of birds and flowers in close-up; wall hangings made from Bardsey wool, socks and hats; small felted bags, willow baskets, enamelled shapes on flat stones, jewellery, bookmarks and cards with pressed wild flowers. The theme is *beauty for ashes* – things created out of found objects, like bottles and driftwood washed up on the shore. Jack likes the concept and also a lot of what is on offer – plenty to choose from to take back for his children, some token of his own passage from despondency to hope.

Jack gets his camera and trekking pole, packs a couple of apples, a Kit Kat and a bottle of boiled water, even his waterproofs – island weather can change so fast. He'll walk down to the café so he can watch the visitors arrive. Strolling down the track, he sees the yellow boat pull into the landing place and Alun begin the process of hauling it up the slipway. Jack turns off to the farm café and sits down at a picnic table. The farmer's wife comes out of the greenhouse in wellies and sweater, hair as always tied with headband.

"Coffee before the rush hour?" she laughs. Was she ever downcast, wondered Jack? She has that cheerfulness and sense of certainty, clear complexion and bright eyes Jack always saw in nuns. A sense of being chosen, maybe, of being blessed. Or just happy to be alive, appreciative of living in this wonderful place. She must be the writer on the beach. She brings his coffee and goes back to the greenhouse.

"Tomatoes to sort," she says.

Jack sees that a small group of visitors has assembled next to the boathouse, two others have already set off to walk along the bay of seals, which are already moaning and complaining, gargling and lamenting. The boat will leave again in four hours, time enough to walk right round the island without rushing. But coffee will be a temptation after the boat trip on the open deck. The group breaks up and starts to amble up the track, three couples and two people on their own. One hangs back, a woman he thinks, maybe watching the seals, maybe just wanting to create a bit of space for herself. The visitors stop to watch the lambs playing. The first couple continues up the track towards the remains of the abbey, but the next two turn in to the farm.

Jack greets them.

"You're really staying here for a week!" exclaims the lady of the couple, early forties, blonde hair, made up, dressed in Berghaus gear. "How wonderful!"

Jack smiles.

"And you have to bring all your provisions?" marvels the blonde. "Is there no Spar shop?"

They troop into the shop, having ordered coffee and flapjacks and come out with bags of presents – there is an honesty box in the shop and a school exercise book in which you write down what you have bought. It is only when they leave that Jack notices the woman down at the boathouse begin to walk up the track. He wants to look at her through his binos under the pretence of watching a swallow fly by but thinks it might look rude. As she walks between the huge stone gateposts and the banked walls he can only see her head. The two couples disappear around the corner and then the lone woman turns in towards the farm.

She is bare-headed, dark-haired, wears an open purple waterproof jacket, with a daysack on her back. She walks easily, not dawdling to watch the lambs in the maternity field, or striding out to start a circuit of the island. She is looking down at her feet on the rough track. He watches her approach, wonders if she will continue past the farm buildings up the mountain path or whether she will turn into the craft shop, whether she will greet him as she passes. For a nanosecond something inarticulate registers in his brain, some familiarity with her form and walk, the momentary flash of a memory. Then she looks up at him, only twenty yards away now. And smiles at him.

It's her. Branwen. His breath catches, his heart hammers. He still sits at the picnic table with his hands around his coffee mug, staring. She turns towards him and he struggles to stand up, shifts his backside round but can't quite swing his booted foot over the bench quickly. He leans back to get a better angle. And that is when he feels her hand touch him on the shoulder.

"Don't get up," she laughs. "It's obviously an effort."

Her fingers on his shoulder, her cheerful voice – as if she'd seen him only yesterday. So casual. He looks up at her, still awkward, confined by the table. She is looking down at him with her soft eyes. She leans forward and kisses him on the lips, soft as four years ago, soft as thirty years ago. The same scent of her skin.

"May I join you?" she asks. "Or are you spoken for?"

"What!" Jack stutters.

"Is there someone in the craft shop who you are waiting for? Will I be an embarrassment? Should I go?"

Jack looks up at her, bewildered.

Branwen moves to the other side of the table.

"I take it that's three 'no's and I can buy you another coffee?"

She slings off her daysack and sits down. The farmer's wife comes out of the greenhouse again.

"The boat wasn't too bumpy, I hear, and you've got a lovely day," she says.

"I have indeed," says Branwen. "Riding my luck. Two coffees please and two flapjacks. The sea air has made me peckish."

"Decaffeinated," mutters Jack, aware it is only the second word he's said since Branwen's arrival.

The farmer's wife goes off and he looks over the table at Branwen.

"I thought I'd give you a surprise," she says. "I think I succeeded. What a lovely place this is. You always could find

161

them: beautiful, isolated places. I remember you always loved islands."

Jack is only just beginning to accept that she is here, sitting opposite him, within touching distance. She must have stayed overnight somewhere and booked her place on the boat. So long since he has seen her, heard her voice on the phone, and here she is, sitting so naturally, so at ease with herself while his dodgy heart beats fast and he wonders how his voice sounds. He takes a deep breath.

"You've completely knocked me out, Branwen." How he loves saying her name to her. "Why now? I don't understand. What's it about?"

Unbidden, the thought comes that her husband has died or that she is leaving him. Dreadful thoughts. But she doesn't look as if either of those things have happened. She looks happy.

"Aren't you glad to see me then?"

"It's like a dream. Of course I'm glad to see you, I'm overwhelmed, I suppose. You're, I don't know, manna from heaven."

"Well, it is supposed to be a holy island," she laughs again. The smile and mischievous eyes have not changed. How quickly they displace his moroseness and introspection. She still captivates him.

"But how have you managed it?" asks Jack. "I presume your husband doesn't know."

"No, of course Hugh doesn't know. I came away with a friend who's back in Caernarvon and she'll cover for me if necessary. But it won't be. You know Hugh trusts me."

Jack knows. Hugh is just too bloody virtuous.

"Your text came out of the blue," continues Branwen, "after more than three years of silence, as you know. I couldn't stop thinking about it. It seemed there might be an opportunity, a last opportunity."

She bites into her flapjack.

"For what? To meet me?"

"That, yes, but more." She takes a drink of coffee then pauses. "I felt I owed you something after all these years, an explanation. Just like you thought you owed me an apology. Almost five years ago you came to see me about that."

"But an explanation for what?"

"For my lack of communication," says Branwen.

"But you explained that. I'll never forget that text you sent me when I was on the train home from Manchester – after that appalling day when it all went wrong."

"I remember it too, you know. I remember saying goodbye on that bench by the canal and hurrying to the bridge. I didn't want to give myself the chance to change my mind. You never came after me."

"I watched you. You never even looked back. I was desperate for you to look back," says Jack.

"And you don't know how much I wanted to. It would have been so easy, to run back and hold you."

They are silent for a moment, each taking a drink of coffee.

"But I didn't."

"No," says Jack. "And then came your text. *I want to feel safe again,* you texted. *What had I been doing there?*"

"I remember. I felt so frightened, bewildered, too."

"You couldn't be two persons, you said, one with Hugh and another with me. You couldn't live two lives, you couldn't deceive. You had to be able to be straight and open again. You had a good life together. You loved him."

Jack feels his voice becoming emotional as he speaks. Branwen's hand is resting on the table just inches from his. He wants to hold it but resists, afraid that yet again what he is feeling is not being reciprocated.

"And I was right. It was the only decision I could make," says Branwen, looking straight into Jack's eyes.

"I know, and I admired you for it. That was the terrible

163

contradiction I was trapped in. Loyalty and love and honesty were qualities I loved in you, and they were taking you away from me."

Jack pauses, takes a bite of flapjack to steady himself. For a moment he sees the scene from outside, wonders if this emotion in him is real, or if, being conscious of it as it happens, there is something of a performance in it?

"But we know all this," he continues. "You know, Branwen, I sometimes curse myself for being too much of a gentleman, too much of a wimp. You made the right decision for the right reasons. I loved and respected you for that."

And now he does take hold of her hand, her warm fingers responding and intertwining with his.

"But sometimes, too, I wish I'd just swept you off your feet, and we'd flowed with all that natural intensity we both felt."

He squeezes her hand hard.

"Those times with you were some of the richest days of my life," he ends.

"I know, mine too," says Branwen softly.

"And we didn't even sleep together," says Jack. "I held back. Crazy. It was unnatural. But if we did make love, I thought you'd hate me afterwards, and that was the last thing I wanted. But that's all history, Branwen. We've coped and lived our very different lives. Come to terms with it – or, in my case, maybe not."

He lifts her hand and kisses her fingers.

"Why are you here? Don't get me wrong. It's unbelievable that you're here and we're talking and I'm holding your hand. But why?"

"Because there's something more I need to explain. But let's walk."

They agree that they should not climb the mountain. It would be more relaxing to walk to the lighthouse and beyond down to the far south of the island, to the very end. Jack has already been there and knows the path, the small bays and deep gullies where the waves wash in. When they set off, Branwen puts her arm in Jack's. The farmer, passing across a field on his tractor, thinks Jack, must see them as a settled elderly couple. He sighs – regret or amusement or a sense of irony? Perhaps all three, he thinks.

"Go on then," says Jack. "Tell me the rest."

"Do you remember you once told me that I would one day see that episode, those times, as an aberration?"

"Of course I remember. It was my turn to feel lonely and vulnerable. But I also remember your reply: *You will never be an aberration to me, Jack.*"

"That's right."

"But isn't that what I became? I dream of you, you know. Not often but regularly. It's why I look forward to going to sleep. But I've convinced myself you never dream of me. Not only have you consciously dismissed me from your life but I don't even exist any more in your unconscious, or your subconscious, whichever it is. So you don't dream of me. And that is the final rejection."

Branwen halts. Wanting a denial, Jack registers that there is driftwood on the stony beach and two seal heads are watching them out in the bay.

"Oh, Jack! That's why I decided to come. Your text was so sad. You were walking and staying where we had walked and stayed thirty years ago. It was like a final pilgrimage, a laying to rest, a death even. That's what I thought. That time with you was so rich, never before and never since have I felt like that. It is still such a powerful memory for me when I allow it to be. And yes, I do sometimes dream of you. Lying next to my sleeping husband, I wake grasping for that dream of you that is already slipping away."

"Is that the truth? I don't want any bullshit."

"Yes, Jack, it is true. I'm here to tell you the truth. I don't know what you want to hear. I don't really know what you've wanted of me all these years since we met again in that café in Swansea."

"I always had a very real sense that you were ending the contact," Jack says, "didn't want it to continue."

"That is correct. I was always brusque. But the question is: why? That's what I'm here to tell you. You remember it was me that ended all communication."

"Will I ever forget it? You saying that as you walked out of the café, the last words you spoke to me until today."

Jack starts walking again, his hands deliberately thrust into his pockets.

"I had to choose, Jack. And I chose my husband and my children, familiarity, safety. But I also chose love – I love Hugh now as much as ever. And he needs me, needed me. He was so jealous of you, knew that what we had had been very special, that for me you had been a romantic, beguiling, dynamic figure."

Jack laughs. "A morose bugger, too. How all things change!"

"Every time I emailed you – even about the simplest things like a holiday or a book – he became tense. He never said anything, would never restrict me or ask me to stop. He gave me my freedom, even though I knew he was scared. He knows we had a passion for each other. When I went to the restaurant to meet you and have dinner with you, he was terrified that passion would ignite again."

"Well, he was right there. It did, but we controlled it," interrupts Jack, irritated by the apparent saintliness of this man.

"He would be frightened now if he knew we were together. He believes that even though we're so much older, that passion could light up again. So back then – and now – I have to protect him, because I love him."

"But, Branwen, I've always understood and accepted that."
She holds his arm and stops him, holds both his hands and looks at him. He sees her eyes, intense and bright.

"Let's sit down," she says.

They find a grassy place where they can sit and lean their backs against the rocks. A lobster boat is doing the rounds of pots just offshore.

"What I have to tell you is that I had to cut you out because I believe and know it too. It could flare if we let it. My husband has been my lifelong love and will continue to be. But you, Jack, have been my one passion – nothing like it before or since. Hugh knows that and has learned to live with it. Does that not say something about the generosity, the maturity of the man? We never speak about it, of course, but we both know. So I keep you always in a corner of my mind, a jewel wrapped in velvet. That's what I've come to tell you."

Jack looks at her. It is what he has dreamed so many times of hearing: that reassurance that it had been and still is real. Now here she is saying it at last. But where is his desire for her? He feels tender towards her, affectionate. Why does nothing stir now? Because he is sixty-seven? Because of the bromide of repeated disappointments? Because of the unexpectedness?

"I don't know whether that's important to you any more, Jack. You have maybe relegated it, even dismissed it, as a way of coping. And I will understand that. But whatever you've done and whatever you feel now, that's what I feel. I wanted you to know. You will always have that special place in my heart – as real as my love for my husband. I treasure you and our time together."

Jack lets the words soak in. He closes his eyes and feels the warmth of the sun on his face, hears the waves in the rocks, the piping of oystercatchers, wailing of seals. Branwen's words are a balm, a healing. But he seems at one remove from the peace they bring, as if he is spectating, even adjudicating. He smells her scent, senses the warmth of her body next to him and yet he is apart from her. Does she feel his response?

Branwen continues: "Over the years you will have doubted what I've just said. I was sorely tempted by you. You were always different, Jack. It took time, a lot of effort and understanding, for my marriage to mend after your reappearance even though, as you know, I was never unfaithful."

"Not even adultery of the mind?"

"Of course, adultery of the mind. But tell me someone who isn't guilty of that. I suspect even Hugh fancies one of his old girlfriends. But he would never act on it."

Jack is listening closely but still spots a gannet heading south, far out at sea.

"When I got your text saying you were coming to Bardsey I knew this was an opportunity I could not miss to make my peace with you. I wanted both my men to be happy. Those years ago, when you reappeared, you came to apologise, you said, for how you had so brutally rejected me, cast me off. Now it's my turn to reappear – not to apologise, for I have nothing to apologise for – but to explain. More than explain – confirm, announce, even proclaim to you."

Jack has not turned to her or taken hold of her hand. He has not stirred.

"Of course, I may have got it all wrong. All this may not matter to you any more. I may just be being ridiculous."

Jack hears a pathos in her voice. Still looking down at the rushing sea, he says: "Not matter? I have thought of you every single day. Living on my own, I have time. I'm not busy like you. I have thought of you a lot here, trying to summarise things, lay them to rest. Without you I have been incomplete this last four years."

Then Branwen takes his hands and kisses them.

"Is this a completion?" she says. "I want it to be. Not a

closure, a completion – a confirmation from you that we still share this, that it is significant for both of us, although it must still remain secret."

Jack looks at her, the face that he has envisaged and remembered so many times. Her hair has touches of grey now, there are the first signs of wrinkles on her neck, lines at the corners of her eyes. But her skin is still smooth, her cheeks soft, her teeth white and even, her lips so sensual.

"How long are you here for?" he asks.

"Just the day trip – we have four hours on the island." She looks at her watch. "Two hours left."

Jack strokes her face. "Just two hours."

"I'm afraid so."

"And I cannot persuade you to stay overnight?"

"It's not possible, Jack, I'm sorry."

She would hate it, anyway: the primitive cottage with no shower or bath, an outside chemical toilet, the inadequate Calor gas heater. Branwen likes warmth and home comforts. So she is still in control, deciding when he can have crumbs from the table. Even as he feels the resentment rise in him he kisses her lips softly. She responds but he pulls gently back and stands up.

"So what happens next?" he asks.

"You're angry, aren't you?" she says, looking up at him.

"No."

But he is. Does her reassurance just disguise the fact he is, again, dancing to her tune? He sighs, stretches out his arm and helps her up. He puts his arms round her.

"I'm not angry. Gobsmacked, perhaps. Resigned, fatalistic – but that's just me, as you know too well. Is this the last post then? You scramble onto that odd yellow boat, sail around Pen Cristin and that's it – our last ever contact?"

"Would it not be better that way? We have made our peace, haven't we? We have confirmed we have each other in the corners of our mind, always. Is that not the most and best we can have?"

They are walking now in the direction of the lighthouse, its square red and white structure with its flashing light dominating this end of the island.

"Yes, I suppose it is."

But it is not enough. This declaration is not enough. He has been battered and disappointed too often. He is too tired to be enthusiastic about what is to be the final compromise, the last and lasting disappointment.

"It's pathetic, I know," Jack says, "but I always looked forward to a contact with you, however mundane or banal. I always hoped – I don't know for what, maybe for this, for what you've just said. And I am grateful for that. But here you are, actually with me. I hear you, see you, smell you, feel you. You are real again, not virtual or imagined. It's too much that I have this for a few hours and then it is taken away again."

Then he turns and puts his arms round her, their heads side by side. He feels her arms hold him. Then he kisses her deeply and she kisses him back, responds immediately. They hold their bodies close to each other and both feel his erection rise against her.

"You see, it is real, after all," he says.

"Feels like it," she says, laughing. "Not bad for an old man!"

They walk on, Jack's erection shrinking. It has been his natural response to her, his body speaking in shorthand for all his emotions and thoughts. Listen to your body, he had been told, it will signal your limitations and your capabilities. Well, his body has spoken – after all these limp, fallow, self-abusive years. But it has been a pointless message, sad and poignant. God knows, his body has signalled his growing limitations over recent years. Now, this last ironic 'hoorah'. He takes a deep breath.

"Maybe it would be best," Jack says, "to agree never to have

170

any more contact at all. That way I would not be checking emails and being disappointed."

"And I would not be feeling bad, having to restrain myself, and knowing that Hugh disliked even this nominal contact."

"So we are agreed?" Jack's voice is dull, defeated.

"I would like us to be... I would like us to be at peace with each other."

"But it is hard, Branwen. I always hoped that I would see you again. To know for certain that this is the last time I will see you and hear you – it is unbearable."

"I feel the same, you know. It is no easier for me. But knowing is better than always wondering, being anxious."

"Who was it said he could deal with the despair, it was the hope he couldn't cope with? Well, I have no choice. Perhaps I will grow up at last. I should be wise and mature by now and I still feel like an adolescent. Doomed to be a geriatric adolescent. What a fate!"

They find a sheltered spot beneath the lighthouse, looking out to the dim silhouette of the Wicklow mountains. Branwen has brought a small picnic in her daysack. They talk about children and books and holidays in a way they both pretend is normal.

"It's like talking to my hairdresser," says Jack.

"Well, thank you."

They pack away their things. They lie back in the sun on their sides and spend a long time just looking into each other's eyes, each seeing the other's moisten. Nothing more is said about their pact. Then Branwen looks at her watch and it is time to return to the boat. Hand in hand they wander back to the landing place. The others are already waiting. One final brief kiss and a nod, a smile. He watches her and the other day-visitors climb aboard the boat then sits on the bench by the boathouse while the boat reverses out of the inlet landing place. Branwen stands in the boat looking at him, waving constantly. He waves back. And then she is round the corner of the crag and only the boat's white wake is to be seen. Jack watches that fade, too, until the sea is smooth and unbroken. It seems like the end of a life.

The late afternoon is still warm. He does not want to return to the cottage yet. Instead he slowly climbs up to the grassy plateau where the remains of hut circles are supposed to be. It is a sheltered place and he sits down leaning against a large rock. From here he can see the whole of the south end of the island where he has just walked with Branwen.

Never to see, or hear, or hear from her again. For the last four years he has sustained what had amounted to a courtly love for her: his celibacy, a weird kind of fidelity to her while she slept in her husband's bed. Anyone else would call him a fool, an old fool. Is he?

This morning he noticed the yellow petals of the daffodils outside the cottage door were already turning brown and dry, papery thin, beginning to crumble. Everything has its brief time. It seems a pity. But the daffodils would renew. For him and Branwen, this is the end. For years with minimum nourishment he has sustained his… his what? Love, he has called it. But is it? Can real love exist on such thin gruel? Has he created a fantasy, a fiction? Perhaps she has been no more than the imaginary friend of childhood, the confidante of fears and wishes; perhaps she has been just "cloff" – like Megan's comfort cloth that she had sucked and chewed as a young child when she was tired or worried or sometimes just happy.

All this time he has believed that he and Branwen could have made a real relationship: thirty years ago they had been so close but the time had been wrong and he had been stupid; four years ago that immediacy had been there again, so strong it could not be doubted. There is something between them: a passion, yes, but more than that, a compatibility. Now he doubts that. She would never have holidayed on Bardsey. She likes her comforts too much: the expensive restaurants, top-of-the-range cruises, business-class flights, ostentatious spending on presents, a constant social whirl, even a preference for hot sunny climes. None of this tallies with his own choices and styles. He likes solitude, she avoids it. He knows there is an adventurousness in her, perhaps more than in himself, but it has been cribbed and confined with her husband who is careful and cautious. Perhaps that sense of adventure would have flourished with him. They would have grown differently. Anyway, it matters not any more. All that is over.

He looks at the white breakers on the blue sea; there is a tanker on the horizon. Even up here he can hear the seals complaining. All these years he has waited, wanting to hear from her some kind of acknowledgement and today she has given it – a passion, like a secret jewel wrapped in velvet. A confirmation. But he is not joyful: the words he has waited for have not worked their magic. He feels empty and hollow. In the end, romantic longing is, by definition, unsatisfiable and, despite the agreed pact, he knows he still hopes to see her. That hope will abide within him like another debility he has to live with. In this too he is now disappointed – the final piece in the jigsaw of his inadequacy.

He looks down at the sandy beach with the bird hide where he had decided to walk into the sea and be borne away with the currents. Then he looks behind him to the rocky crest at the top of the mountain where he had decided to live. What now is left? He will continue in the slow decline of age, lonely, lonesome. He does not have the courage to bring about his own death. Maybe later, he tells himself, when he is an anxiety to his children, dribbling and confused and needing carers to check his medication and make sure he's turned the gas stove off, treating himself with dark chocolate. Maybe then, having arranged to donate his body to a teaching hospital in a last

173

effort to be useful, he will find a way to end his humiliation. Until then he will carry on: learn more about birds, enjoy his children, celebrate Kathy. Perhaps, as he grows more sedentary, he will press wild flowers, learn to identify graveyard lichen (or something similarly melancholy, he grunts a laugh at the thought), build a model railway landscape as he had as a boy, with chicken wire and papier mâché. Return to childhood.

And always with forlorn hope, with bright sadness for the possibility of things.

He stands up, too quickly, for he is for a moment or two light-headed. He bends for his trekking pole, looks out to the west again, and starts down the hill.

EPILOGUE

Jack carried out the white plastic chair and placed it firmly on the snow-covered decking of the fisherman's hut. He placed a small matching picnic table next to the chair. Finally he put on the table his two packets of sleeping pills and painkillers, his bottle of rich golden Laphroaig whisky, a quarter already drunk, and his iPod. Standing, he looked out over the black sea that lapped up under the refurbished hut with a gentle slapping noise; the pitch black of a moonless night, the first hints of the Northern Lights flickering in the sky. He breathed in the pure salty air, felt the icy cold on his face. But his body was warm – why suffer unnecessarily? He wore two pairs of thick socks in his well-worn walking boots, thermal long johns and padded trousers, two fleeces and a quilted jacket. His woolly headband protected his ears, the hood of his jacket was pulled over his head. He might be two hundred miles north of the Arctic Circle on an early December night in the Norwegian Lofoten islands – and alone – but he wanted to be comfortable and at ease. Three years ago on another island he had dithered as he laughably put himself on trial. There were to be no further adjournments now: the medical man had put on the black cap.

Jack sat down. How fitting, he mused, that this concluding act of his life had been precipitated by an incident so absurdly mundane. One evening, watching football on the TV (another looming Arsenal defeat), he had reached for his mug of coffee and knocked the remote control from the arm of his chair. As he stretched quickly down to pick it up he had a mini-stroke – what the hospital later told him was a 'TIA': a transient ischemic attack. Although he had immediate difficulty in speaking – the left side of his mouth seemed numb – he had managed to phone for an ambulance. Rapidly transferred from A&E, a stroke consultant had arranged an ultrasound scan of his carotid artery, which supplied oxygenated blood through the neck to the brain. It was eighty per cent furred up.

"Without surgery," the young, confident consultant had said, peering at the computer screen, "a complete blockage is likely."

"And if that happened?" asked Jack.

"Almost certainly a totally disabling stroke, or even the end."

With me in a nursing home, having my arse wiped for me and being fed with a spoon, thought Jack.

"Surgery is possible," continued the consultant, "a sort of pipe-cleaning procedure to reduce the risk but I have to tell you that with your irregular heartbeat and leaking heart valves the operation itself could cause such a stroke rather than prevent it."

So no joy there, then. A rock and a hard place.

"I'll think about it," said Jack. "Thank you for your honesty."

Back at home, Jack took stock. He had three choices: sit on the sofa, live cautiously, making sure the TV remote was securely at hand, but knowing that even so a stroke could occur at any moment; or continue walking the hills but with a higher risk of a sudden, severe stroke; or call it a day and pre-empt the stroke. He'd always had a fear and loathing of being severely crippled, no dignity left and a burden to others.

It was odd how the first things that came to mind were practicalities: cancel the renovation of the conservatory, recycle the brochures for next summer's holiday; forget about tickets for the next Rugby World Cup. With some surprise Jack had felt himself relaxing into peace of mind, experiencing a feel-good factor: his uncertainty and fear would be over, his children would not be responsible for him. He smiled to himself: after all, he would be more useful to his children dead than alive – they could pay off their mortgages. He was a free man, free to cut his losses, avoiding pain and dependence – but working to a deadline.

For a week around the September equinox – that autumn fulcrum of the year – he and his children and grandchildren had holidayed in a farmhouse near Aberdaron. They had walked the walks now familiar to four generations of his family, they had driven to the headland and looked out to Bardsey. On the equinox itself, the last Friday, when his grandchildren were in bed, he had opened bottles of the best champagne, explained his medical condition and his decision to Abi, Tom and Megan. He had been calm and determined: nothing they could say, he made plain, would make him change his mind. It was for the best, it was sensible. Of course, after the shock, they had protested and there had been tears. But it was what he wanted, he said: to make an end of it before he became a dribbling cripple. Life's due process – we are born astride the grave. There would be dignity in a death of his own choosing. With their agreement, he signed the papers to leave his cadaver to a teaching hospital. There would be a party, not a funeral.

He had hugged them all, especially Megan, because Megan would now have no parents. But she was twenty-three years old now, already successfully established in her career and in a relationship with a good, gentle boyfriend whom Jack was confident she would marry. He spoke to her alone out in the darkened garden and felt they achieved a kind of peace and understanding.

"I will miss you all," he laughed, "if you know what I mean."

Jack raised his glass of champagne for a final toast. "Think kindly of me, in spite of everything."

Back at home he selected his time and place to shape a satisfying symmetry with Kathy's death. He made arrangements, booking his flight tickets via Oslo to Bodo, his ferry to Lofoten and his accommodation there. He had decided on the date – Kathy's birthday, when fortunately there would be no moon – and the place: Lofoten, because it was the most beautiful place he had ever been to and would be cold and snowy, as when Kathy died. All his life he had wanted to see the Northern Lights – he had seen films and been overwhelmed by their beauty. With luck, they would be the last thing he would witness in this beautiful world.

There had been no contact with Branwen since their meeting on Bardsey. He decided not to tell her what he was doing. If he told her, she would be either indifferent or sad. In either case, what was the point? Had she told him the truth on Bardsey, that he had been her one passion? Or had her words been a kindly meant consolation, to make them both feel better? Over the last three years his feelings for her had moved from disappointment with periods of resentment to a resigned sadness. But never indifference.

The emotional churning which had filled his life had stilled at last but that didn't mean he understood any more about it. Yes, there had been two brief periods of reality with Branwen – their first affair, and their reunion. There had been excitement, adventure, immediacy, sensuality, compatibility. He would always believe there had been some goodness in it. But also he had greedily needed from Branwen a kind of validation, a love and acceptance that covered his failures and inadequacies and filled some vacancy in him. In a way, she had compelled him to make it all into a fiction. And why? Then had he elevated her into an imaginary wish-fulfilment, memories embellished to create a fantasy? Because it was easier than dwelling on the reality of Kathy, the waste and tragedy of her life. *We tell ourselves stories in order to go on living.*

Kathy was too much of a loss, her absence too keen for himself and Megan. At birthdays, Christmas, family gatherings, on holidays, her vivacity and enthusiasm were too obviously missing. Most difficult of all had been the knowledge of Megan's growing up that Kathy had taken to her grave: what her first words were, when she took her first steps, her first discoveries and skills, anecdotes Jack had forgotten. All this was irreplaceable. Whatever he had later felt about Branwen, Kathy had been the reality: his wife, the mother of his daughter. He had felt passion for them both, but both had been snatched away.

Now he had just a couple of hours to live. He was warm and snug. He filled his glass with whisky, sniffed it, held the glass up to the darkness in a kind of toast and took a generous drink. He swallowed the first half dozen sleeping pills one by one, calm now and content. True happiness in his life had been with Kathy and Megan, Abi and Tom. Sometimes with Kathy, lying in bed with her after making love, or lying on the grass in the sun after a long walk, words redundant, he sensed that fellowship more quiet even than solitude, a solitude made perfect with her. But happiness was always temporary and illusory. Struggling, coping, coming to terms – that was what life was about. Most people muddled through. He certainly had done. His one constancy was his love for his children, but even that had been necessarily flawed by his part-time fatherhood after the divorce. Branwen had been a dream, a recurring dream. In spite of the differences between them, he still believed they could have been soulmates, good for each other. But he had spurned the reality all those years ago, and second chances don't come. The dream for him had been enriching and beautiful, a hope; for her, it had become shameful, a regret. That was the essential sadness, the absurdity. In the end, Branwen had been ashamed not of her treatment of himself, Jack, but of her husband.

Jack took another drink and more pills. No benign wisdom touched him with grace but it was time at last to stop lacerating himself. He had not been deliberately cruel. He was inadequate and incomplete, yes, but that was who he was. The loving is more important than its fulfilment – so they say. Well, he has loved, perhaps not too wisely or too well, but in his own flawed way. And now this was the end. On the table inside the hut was his neatly written letter of explanation with contact telephone numbers. The hotel staff would find it when he didn't come over for breakfast in the morning. Also on the table was the wooden tetrahedron he had carried on his pilgrimage – the Platonic solid symbolising harmony within folly. He remembered gathering scraps each day on the walk: a pebble, a tuft of wool, a pine cone, a dog whelk. He couldn't recall the fifth. His life had been follies within the harmony around him.

He settled back, the whisky rasping his throat then giving him more warmth in his chest, his head muzzing peacefully. He plugged in his earphone from the iPod. He had selected Enya. He turned up the sound so that it filled his head. Enya, Kathy dancing, Abi and Tom and Megan: they were all together in Jack's head.

Rising in the east came Venus: the bane and pleasure of his life. He laughed: the final piece of the jigsaw. And now the lights were billowing across the sky in great green scarves and streamers, never still, swirling, dancing, dancing, dancing. It was music made visible. Now at last the beauty and movement of the lights that flickered above him outshone the inward rays that had pierced him with such scrutiny. Peace at last. *All that survives of us is love,* he had read. Was it true?

"Kathy," he whispered. "Kathy."

Then his eyelids droop and his glass falls from his hand, silently landing on the snow, its white crystals stained dark by the golden whisky. Above him charged particles are flaring out from the sun, blown by the solar wind to spiral along the Earth's magnetic field lines in a ring around the North Pole, the atmosphere glowing with their energy.

Jack sleeps. Then clouds move in, the lights fade and are hidden. It begins to snow again. Flakes land softly on Jack's sleeping form, at first dissolving as they touch his blue jacket, then slowly clustering, accumulating into a white layer while the skin of his face tightens with ice and his heart slows to a stop.

AUTHOR'S NOTE

M y partner Jan and I walked the Pilgrim's Way and spent a week on the wonderful island of Bardsey. I could not have done the walk without her. "It was a l ovely walk," she says, "and now you've spoilt it with this: so depressing for me to read." (But I was not contemplating these matters on the actual walk nor sitting in the bird hide considering suicide.) On the other hand, a friend – not relative – Martin Roberts describes the book as a "searingly vivid depiction of regret and guilt". Perhaps it's both.

The four 'contemplations' are derived from episodes in my life but refracted through a seriously malfunctioning memory, augmented by my imagination and adapted to the narrative themes.

The story of Branwen, the third element of the novel, was seeded by articles about some of the consequences of Friends Re-united. John Banville's *Ancient Light* encouraged me to play further with ideas about how what really happens can be blurred by selective recollection and even wish-fulfilment.

The book is therefore a work of fiction.